"I HAVEN'T THANKED YOU YET, HAVE I?" HE WHISPERED.

Before Bethany could think or draw breath, Griff had drawn her into the circle of his arms. She gasped at the shock of bare flesh against bare flesh. Then his mouth came down on hers, slow and sensuous and knowing every nuance of her lips. At her back, his hands moved knowingly, purposefully, unfastening the towel that covered her, lightly smoothing the line of her back, over her still-clothed hips, her bare thighs.

She sighed in acknowledgment of the flame that was sweeping through her. She could feel her body's movement, as wild as the drumbeat of her heart. . . .

FRANCINE SHORE has been a writer since the age of 14, when she sold her first story. Born in Japan, she has lived with her husband and two sons in Bangkok, Thailand, as well as in diverse parts of the United States. Besides being a full-time writer, she has worked on a newspaper and had her own DJ show. She now teaches creative writing to both adults and young people. Her previous Rapture Romances are *Flower of Desire*, *The Golden Maiden*, *Love's Gilded Mask*, and *Lover in the Wings*.

Dear Reader:

We at Rapture Romance hope you will continue to enjoy our four books each month as much as we enjoy bringing them to you. Our commitment remains strong to giving you only the best, by well-known favorite authors and exciting new writers.

We've used the comments and opinions we've heard from you, the reader, to make our selections, so please keep writing to us. Your letters have already helped us bring you better books—the kind you want—and we appreciate and depend on them. Of course, we are always happy to forward mail to our authors—writers need to hear from their fans!

Happy reading!

The Editors
Rapture Romance
New American Library
1633 Broadway
New York, NY 10019

LOVER'S RUN

by

Francine Shore

RAPTURE ROMANCE
NEW AMERICAN LIBRARY

PUBLISHER'S NOTE

This novel is a work of fiction. Names, characters, places, and incidents either are the product of the author's imagination or are used fictitiously, and any resemblance to actual persons, living or dead, events, or locales is entirely coincidental.

NAL BOOKS ARE AVAILABLE AT QUANTITY DISCOUNTS
WHEN USED TO PROMOTE PRODUCTS OR SERVICES.
FOR INFORMATION PLEASE WRITE TO PREMIUM MARKETING DIVISION,
NEW AMERICAN LIBRARY, 1633 BROADWAY,
NEW YORK, NEW YORK 10019.

Copyright © 1984 by Francine Shore

All rights reserved

SIGNET, SIGNET CLASSIC, MENTOR, PLUME, MERIDIAN AND NAL BOOKS
are published by New American Library,
1633 Broadway, New York, New York 10019

First Printing, July, 1984

1 2 3 4 5 6 7 8 9

PRINTED IN THE UNITED STATES OF AMERICA

Chapter One

❧

"Bethany Sheridan? We've got business to discuss!"

The tall, broad-shouldered stranger standing by the swinging kennel's gate had a distinctive voice. It wasn't overly loud, and yet Bethany could hear each word he said clearly over the barking and whining complaints of her forty dogs and the insistent sounds made by the north wind. She couldn't see his face at this distance, but she could certainly sense his determination and purpose.

She had been kneeling in the snow examining Katiktok's paws while Freya lapped her cheek. Now she straightened slowly. She registered the fact that her visitor's expensive parka and heavy ski pants looked new and that the snowmobile parked near her cabin was also new and costly. A *cheechako*? she wondered. But what was a tenderfoot doing fifty miles away from Anchorage and "civilization"?

"I'm Bethany Sheridan," she called back. "What business brings you to this part of Alaska to see me?"

"My name is Griffith Deane—Griff, to my friends. I want to talk about the musher's life with you and perhaps buy some of your dogs. I've learned that you're not only a champion racer but also that you raise the best sled dogs around."

It wasn't so unusual for someone to seek her out like this. With dogsled racing rising sharply as a new sport, several thousand dogsled enthusiasts—

5

mushers—participated annually in the more than sixty events scattered up and down the racing circuit. But why did this man's name stir her memory? Bethany narrowed her dark eyes as he walked closer and she took in details about him that nudged remembrance. At least six feet, she thought; with those shoulders, probably more. Dark hair, almost black under the parka hood. A lean, dark, high-cheekboned face, proud, aquiline nose, a long-lipped, mobile mouth. I've seen that face before. I know I have. Where?

He seemed to reach into her mind and read the thought. "Laconia." He slid his parka hood back and smiled as her eyes widened in complete recognition. "You won the race and I placed third."

She remembered now. Of course! She had not had the time to do more than shake his hand after that race; he had left too quickly. Yet she remembered vividly the warm grip of his congratulating handshake, the way sunlight had glinted on eyes as completely and intently green as young spring leaves.

Even in the flush of her victory, her response to his look and touch had surprised her.

"You and the second place winner had an almost perfect photo finish," she said, trying to gloss over her reaction. "I remember people saying you were a beginner. The track was terrible that day, and many experienced mushers quit early on. You did very well."

He held out a gloved hand, gave hers a leisurely shake. "But you won," he pointed out. "That's why I've come to see you, Bethany. I want to win the Rohn Relay this December. To do that I'm going to need the best dogs, the best advice, and the best partner available. I've been referred to you by Julie Kobuk. I'm boarding with her family in Tilikit."

"You *are* serious!" she exclaimed. He simply

nodded, waiting. Anyone who would board in the little Indian village of Tilikit, population 150, had to mean business. And if Julie had sent him to her, she could do nothing but oblige. "The Kobuks are my closest friends," she told Griff Deane cordially. "Of course I'll help you. Come and look over my dogs. I've just returned from our daily run, and I'm about to feed them."

He stepped through the kennel door and walked in among the dogs. Bethany noted that he remained relaxed and easy as they came to sniff and take in this new human scent. "They're Alaskan huskies, aren't they?" he asked. "You don't go in for Siberian huskies or malamutes?"

She shook her head. He was fondling Katiktok's ears, and her favorite lead dog was licking his hand already. A fast worker, Griff Deane, she thought, then felt an odd tensing as his green eyes looked up into hers. "I don't think Siberians are fast enough even though they have great stamina. And my feeling is that malamutes can often be surly." She rubbed exuberant Aladin's ears as she added, "I only race fifteen of these dogs, but I'm constantly training replacements for my team. Any dogs you choose would do you proud."

"I'm sure you're right." He watched interestedly as she went about feeding the animals with a meal of broth, beef, and vitamins. She was competent, all right—as quick and as sharp as he remembered from the New Hampshire race—and attractive, too, in spite of the layers of Arctic clothing. But did she have the stamina for the grueling Rohn Relay? "I take it you've been in training for some time?" he probed.

"Of course. It's a relatively new event, good training for the Iditarod in early March. But while the Iditarod goes over more than a thousand miles, the relay will only cover the distance from Settlers Bay to Rohn." She finished her feeding, faced him. "Julie Kobuk was right, you know. You're going to need not only the best dogs and equipment but a good racing partner. I've been giving a lot of thought to that myself, and I could give you one or two names—"

He cut her short. "I was thinking more along the lines of us partnering each other. From what I saw at Laconia I'd say you were as good a racer as any."

Bethany was thrown off balance by his words, and she saw he knew it. His smile widened to show strong white teeth, and she was certain he was confident about her answer. She resented both this smugness and her own confusion. "I'm flattered," she said, struggling to keep a defensive note out of her voice. "I think a partnership would be premature, though. You've only seen me race once, and I know you're a novice."

There was no impatience in his many-timbred voice, only conviction. "Everyone has to be a beginner at one time or another. And since Laconia was the first race I'd competed in, third prize didn't seem so bad. Since then, I've perfected my technique, practiced a great deal, and feel confident that I can win the Rohn Relay. However, I need a team. The team I have been using is, I feel, entirely unsuited to Alaskan racing." His lean face was suddenly amused. "Winning also depends on the right partner, of course. And as partners go you aren't exactly reassuring. How tall are you, Bethany? Five foot two?"

"I'm five five," she said tersely.

"Really?" She was small-boned, he thought, her features delicate under red-gold brows that matched her hair. Her dark eyes showed spirit and something else—a warning. It was as if a barrier had been thrown up against expected attack. Why? he wondered. "I'd imagine you're also about a hundred and fifteen pounds dripping wet. If we're talking about the weaknesses of a partner, that might be considered a liability. Racing calls for muscle and strength and stamina as well as skill." Her eyes were unfriendly, and he couldn't help adding, "No doubt you're peerless in other, er, endeavors."

She could guess at what he was doing, and his tactics both irritated and amused her. He was trying to rile her into defending her fitness as a partner in the relay. He wanted to trick her into accepting his offer.

"I'm sure that you're just as skilled," she replied lightly, and watched the expression in those astonishing eyes change. He seemed intrigued and rather pleased, as if he'd found in her an unexpected match. "However, I like to measure people by their performance."

"Their performance in everything?" There was an edge of insinuation in his voice, but she ignored it.

"Supposing I show you my own team? You did say you wanted the best, and I'd like to show you what champions I've trained."

Like a proud parent, she called her team to her one by one. Katiktok was first. "This one was in the first litter I raised. She's been with me through several big races including ones at Ely and Truckee," she explained. As Katiktok whined softly, she introduced the others: Freya, the other lead dog; the strong, heavy young males Ali and Pushkin; Aladin and reliable Growler. As she spoke of the strengths of her team, she was aware of his intense attention.

"You're saying that a musher is like a coach who allows for the strengths and weaknesses of his players and then capitalizes on them," he said. "How long do you need to run them before you learn their characteristics and how best to deal with them?"

She was surprised at his quickness. "I run my team every day, beginning in September. If you want to

enter the relay, you'd better start training right
away."

"You mean, *we'd* better start training." His intensity dissolved into a smile again. "Seeing that you'll
be my partner, Bethany Sheridan, how much will
you charge me for a team of dogs?"

"I am not your partner," she shot back. "And as far
as the dogs are concerned, they're worth top dollar."
If Griff Deane wanted to dicker, she would be glad to
oblige him. Maybe Julie hadn't told him that she was
a hardheaded businesswoman when it came to her
precious animals.

They hammered a price back and forth for some
time, with Bethany upping Griff's original offer considerably. She had the impression, however, that the
final number was what he had intended to give in the
first place and that he simply had enjoyed the transaction. As she helped him pick out his team, she
watched him unobtrusively. He was quick, he was
strong, and he seemed to have an instinctive feel for
the dogs. She had been impressed with his speed and
style the one time she'd seen him race. And she *had*
been looking for a race partner. Ordinarily, she'd
have welcomed his offer. Why then did she feel this
confusion, this odd tension in his presence?

"Are you considering my offer?" He was watching
her in the northern dusk and smiling, and she
frowned. There was absolutely no reason for this
man to unbalance her as he seemed to do so easily.
She caught her generous bottom lip between her
teeth for a moment, frowning. She was an accepted
equal among the predominately male mushers along
the dogsled racing circuit. Troubled, she looked up at
him and shook her head.

"I'm not sure," she said. "Why don't I think it over
and give you an answer in a day or so?"

He said, promptly, "Why not a week?"

"Why a week?" Katiktok was sidling up to Griff, letting him rub her ears and licking his gloved hand. It certainly looked, Bethany thought wryly, like desertion.

"Don't you think that we'll need at least a week to see whether we're compatible partners?" She opened her mouth to protest but he added swiftly, "Look, it makes sense. Think about it! I've bought your dogs, but I'll need you to familiarize me with the area around here so that I can train them. I've never raced in Alaska before and could certainly use some pointers on the terrain." He paused. "Naturally, I'd insist on paying you for your time."

What he said was reasonable, and yet she hesitated. She felt as if he we pushing her into a position she would do better to avoid. Smoothly, as if he had not sensed her hesitation, he said, "I also want you to look over my sled. I bought it from a fellow in Tilikit—another of Julie's recommendations. And, speaking of Julie, she made it plain that I'd be persona non grata at her table tonight unless I brought you along to share the meal."

His voice was easy; the green gaze he turned on her was not. There was almost something palpable in the directness of his eyes. It took her aback as nothing had in quite a long time. Then, she rallied. She was, after all, twenty-seven and not seventeen. Griff Deane was just another aspiring musher, and she'd trained several would-be racers. Now that she thought it over, the profit she'd make from the sale of the dogs and the lessons she could give him were too good to pass up. It wasn't as if she were made of money.

"A week, then," she said in what she hoped was a pleasant but firm voice. "I'll take you along with me when my team makes its daily run, and what I can,

I'll teach you. And you're right. In a week, we'll definitely know whether we can be partners."

He smiled, but his voice was as decided and as firm as her own. "Oh, we'll be partners," he told her. "Once I see a good thing, I don't let go of it." He slipped an arm through hers adding, "Care to put a side bet on it, Bethany Sheridan?"

Chapter Two

Because the dogs had already been exercised for the day, Bethany chose to ride into Tilikit on Griff Deane's snowmobile. They covered the seven miles to the village in a silence that surprised Bethany. Usually a tenderfoot was eager to learn more about Alaska, quick to ask questions or make comments. Griff Deane did none of these things. He simply drove the powerful machine along until they were almost in Tilikit. Then, he nodded to the severe beauty of the countryside around them.

"This silence and peace is very rare," he commented. "It's something you can't buy at any price."

He actually understood how she herself felt. She felt an odd prickling warmth, a kind of reverse gooseflesh. "That's why I came to live out here," she said. "At that time, my family was still living in New Hampshire, and they thought I was crazy. Since then my folks have relocated to Florida, and now they *know* I'm crazy."

He smiled. "I can see why they'd think that. You're miles away from your nearest neighbor. Not many women would have had the guts to do what you did."

She shrugged. "There are several women that I know of who live as I do. Besides, when I first came here I wasn't alone."

She hadn't meant to tell him that, and she was

annoyed at herself. "Your husband?" he asked, and having said so much she had to answer.

"Fiancé. We met while working a summer job at Mount McKinley National Park. Piers and I were both interested in raising and selling sled dogs, and we both wanted to live out in the wilderness."

"But he tired of the wide open spaces." The glance he shot her was sheathed by the dark, but she could remember the clear green directness of their gaze.

"People change." She did not want to remember how Piers' dreams had changed, how they had diverged from hers. "Our decision was mutual," she went on, wishing she had never brought up the subject. "We parted as good friends."

"I hardly think so." The light of his snowmobile glinted on the sign that said Tilikit as he added, "No man in his right mind would be content simply to be your friend, Bethany Sheridan. And these good-byes are never mutual, are they?"

No doubt he was talking from experience, she thought irritably. The man knew too much! For a second memories crowded in. She could remember the arguments that had begun—Piers tired of the remote cabin, feeling cut off from the rest of the world. "You love the wilderness more than me," he had accused her. "You want your independence more than our love." And perhaps Piers had been right. She had missed him terribly when he left; she had cried for him at night when the bed felt cold and empty without his warmth. Yet, she hadn't wanted him enough to leave the kind of life she loved for his sake.

"Since Piers there's been no one to share your life?" Griff was asking. She shook her head. "It seems a hard life."

"No, it's wonderful. It's the kind of life-style I chose." They swept into a long street that linked scattered wooden houses and made up the village of Tilikit. "What about you? Where do you call home?"

A shrug of the broad shoulders and he said, "New York, I suppose. That's where my company is located, anyway. But I've lived in many other parts of the country—and the world, too, come to that." He grinned at her. "I've been in places that are almost as wide open as Alaska, and in teeming cities that would make your pretty flesh crawl, Beth."

She frowned over this familiar contraction of her name, but before she could comment he had stopped the snowmobile in front of one of the largest houses in the village. It had been newly painted and boasted a brand new roof together with a massive TV antenna. Since the state had installed a great satellite dish beyond the village, the villagers had powered their TV sets by means of a gasoline generator. Bethany grinned as she heard its gruff huffing beyond the village. Everybody in Tilikit enjoyed watching the soaps.

"There's my gear." Griff was pointing to the porch where a sled, harness, and gang-line tethers had been stored with other necessary equipment. "As far as I can tell, the quality is first class."

Bethany was inspecting the sled when Julie Kobuk opened the door of the house. She shouted out loud and enfolded Bethany in her stout arms.

"Bethy!" Julie exclaimed. "Good to see you, dearie! I'm glad this handsome *cheechako* convinced you to come down here and eat with us."

Bethany hugged her friend back. "You know I wouldn't need a second invitation, Julie."

"Got to come more often." Julie gave Bethany a pinch that penetrated the parka she wore and the sweater beneath. "You look too skinny, Bethy. You don't eat more, the men won't run after you."

She winked outrageously at Griff, who was standing some distance from her, and Bethany spoke quickly to forestall comment. "I hear you've been recommending me as a good dog breeder."

"Well, you're the best, aren't you?" She raised her voice. "Elmer! Tony! Giuliana! Look who's come back with Griff!"

The other Kobuks now came out of the house, to hug and shake hands. Small, wiry Elmer welcomed Bethany like a daughter while teen-aged Tony shyly permitted a hug, and small Giuliana toddled between Bethany and Griff and her parents, expressing her joy in a huge smile.

"Come inside and get warm," Elmer urged. Warm was what the Kobuk house was, too. Delicious smells wafted from Julie's kitchen, and heat from the big wood stove filled a large living area that was furnished with many-colored cushions, comfortable furniture, and great, thick fur rugs. Bethany saw Griff being led to the best seat by the stove while Julie pulled her into the kitchen.

"I knew you were looking for a partner for the relay," Julie said. "The minute I saw him, Bethy, I knew he was the one for you." She raised a pudgy finger. "That man's a winner. He doesn't know the word 'lose.' "

"How do you know him?" Bethany asked cautiously.

"Funny thing, *he* got to know us. A man Elmer knows met Griff during a dogsled meet. When he heard Griff wanted to enter the Rohn Relay, he suggested that we might take in a boarder." She added complacently, "Ours is the only house in Tilikit big enough for a *cheechako* to stay in comfortably."

"But why Tilikit? Why not Anchorage or Settlers Bay?"

Julie tilted a bowl of fragrant stew and began to ladle great spoonfuls into bowls. "Like I said, he was looking for a partner for the Rohn Relay. I had a feeling he was looking for you, Bethy."

Bethany looked toward Griff. Though seemingly at his ease near the stove, with Giuliana on his knees and Tony hovering nearby, she had the impression that his attention was centered not on them but on her. "That's silly," she told Julie. "He only saw me race once, in Laconia. He didn't know where I lived."

Julie grinned. "He asked for you by name, anyway. Said you acted like a winner in New Hampshire, and he wanted a winner for a partner. Like I said, he was looking for you."

She called her family and Griff to the big kitchen table, and as they came Bethany stared at the tall, dark-haired stranger. Had he really tracked her down simply to see if she might be the right partner for him in the Rohn Relay? That took money and time. What kind of business was Griff Deane in that he could spare so much money and so much time? He'd mentioned a company in New York, but what did he do?

"May I?" With a courtly grace he held out the rough wooden chair to seat her. She was acutely conscious of his nearness, of the long, powerful line of muscle that rippled across his shoulders and arm and back. Muscle was evident under his expensive woolen shirt and under the ski pants he wore. His hands rested lightly on her arms as he pushed in her chair. For a moment, her pulses leaped at the strangely disturbing touch. Then, he was returning to his own place across the table from her.

"Any news from the company today, Griff?" Elmer was asking as he dipped into the lavish meal of caribou stew, mashed potatoes, and sourdough pancakes.

"Griff keeps in touch with New York via radio." Julie was referring to the local radio station in Raedar, a town to the south of Tilikit. Raedar, together with a post office, emergency medical supply facility, and church, boasted an eight-party phone system, but the phones were unreliable. They constantly broke down in winter, and radio messages were more popular. "He's got to keep tabs on his people at Deane Enterprises somehow."

She spoke as if this explained everything, but Bethany was bewildered. "What exactly is Deane Enterprises?"

"My company. We're an electronics firm providing components to high technology sales industries." Griff spoke offhandedly, but Elmer, who prided himself on having a small portfolio of invested stock, shook his head.

"Bethy, don't let him bamboozle you. Deane is a big concern. Last year I read it acquired Holmes Transportation, which is a big shipping business." He turned to Griff. "What's your latest move, Griff? You folks deciding to take over business in the state of Alaska?"

Griff grinned at Elmer while declining a third helping of sourdough pancakes. "As it happens, we are investigating the possibility of opening a branch office of Deane Enterprises in Anchorage. We have a man there right now who gets messages from New York and then sends them on to me." He paused. "What we're mainly interested in right now is a packaging corporation called Halstead. We've been busy negotiating to acquire it."

"Yet you can take time off to race dogs?" Bethany asked, astonished.

He shrugged. "I've done the initial groundwork for the transaction, and my people are quite capable of following through. A corporation head is seldom needed until a critical stage in negotiations is reached." There was no condescension in his voice, but she felt it anyway; she felt the power and arrogance of so much wealth. He was saying, "The trick in business is to employ the right people. That's a principle that my father dinned into my head when he was still alive. The right people and the right time—that's the key to success. That, and hard work, of course."

What hard work? Bethany wondered. He spoke with enjoyment, even relish. She could very well picture Griff as a business mogul ready to indulge his whims while his people scurried about doing his bidding. He could *afford* to take up dogsled racing or anything else he wanted. Others did the sweating and he reaped the rewards.

"It sounds like a perfect formula," she said.

"It is. I'm glad you agree with me, Bethany." He had placed his hands on Julie's cheerful checkered tablecloth and against the bright background they looked powerful and almost ruthless. "That's why I think we'll be perfect partners in the Rohn Relay. We both enjoy challenge, and we both go out to win. Winning is what life is all about, after all."

"Winning is right." Shy Tony spoke for the first time. "Bethany's a big name around here, Griff. She's the best woman musher since Talka. You know, one of the famous lovers."

"You know about our local legend, don't you?" Elmer asked. Griff shook his head and Bethany sighed inwardly. Now the Kobuks would spend the next two hours detailing the tired old legend of Lover's Run.

But tonight her friends were much too interested in the present to venture back into folklore. "The lovers were legendary dogsled racers," Julie explained briefly. "The area where Bethy lives is named Lover's Run for them." She leaned forward. "You two really going to be partners, then?"

"We've made an agreement to try racing together

for a week." Julie smiled in satisfaction and Bethany could hardly repress a frown. First her favorite dog and now the Kobuks seemed to be falling prey to Griff's easy charm, and this irritated her. She got to her feet. "It's getting late, Julie. Let me help you clean up before I go."

Because she was like family, Julie usually never refused her help. Tonight, however, she shook her head. "You're right, Bethy—it's late and if you're training you'll be up early." She paused. "Griff, you driving Bethy back to her cabin or should Elmer or Tony?"

Griff got up at once. "I'm at Bethany's disposal," he said, and something in the shading of that distinctive voice was unsettling. Bethany wished she had brought her own sled and dogs, then was angry with herself. This was ridiculous. She had agreed to a trial partnership, and they needed to be at ease with each other.

She tried hard to relax on the long ride home, but the silence of the dark night was not a comfortable one. To break it she began to detail a plan for their first day out together. He listened to her conscientiously, and she could see the dark silhouette of his head nod from time to time.

"You say you want to start out early," he finally interrupted her. "What time will be convenient for you?"

"How about five?" If she had planned to shock him, it was a waste of time. He simply nodded.

"As I said before I'm completely at your disposal, Bethany. Anybody who's as good a racer as the legendary Talka deserves my fullest cooperation."

They came to a gliding stop. Some yards away stood the dark upright lines of her cabin, and into the silence of the chill night rose the barking welcome of her dogs. Bethany drew a deep breath of relief. Home, she thought.

Griff cut the snowmobile motor and dismounted. He held out a hand to help her, and because she was not sure that she wanted to take that hand, she stumbled as she rose from the snowmobile seat. For a second she felt her feet slide from under her. The next moment, she was in his arms.

She heard his indrawn breath and realized that he was as startled as she was—but not for long. The strong arms tightened around her, drawing her close. In spite of their protective clothing she was acutely conscious of the hard-muscled body pressing against her softness. In spite of the cold wind and chill night air, she felt suddenly very warm, as if some fire within her had inexplicably come alight.

His mouth was very near hers. Without hurry, it moved, lowered, touched her lips. It was a light kiss, tentative, totally out of sync with the effect that it had on her. She found that she was trembling with the force of her confused feelings, that there was an almost irresistible desire within her to reach out and pull his dark head closer so that her mouth could learn the shape and texture and taste of his.

As if in answer to her mute want, he bent to her lips again. This time there was nothing tentative about the kiss. Boldly, Griff's mouth opened over hers, forcing a like response. With tongue and lips and breath he invaded the inner recesses of her mouth while one hand rose to push back her parka hood and cup the back of her head posessively against its palm.

She couldn't breathe. She could not think. Did not want to—had to! With an effort, she pulled her mouth from his, drew breath, stared up at him with wide eyes.

"Stop," she whispered, and then, "don't ... please!"

She emphasized her words by pushing with both hands against the broad wall of his chest. For a moment his hands held her tight, and then he stepped away.

"Would you prefer to continue our discussion about tomorrow?" he asked. There was a huskiness in the deep voice, already so familiar to her. He raised a hand, and she felt his touch on her hair, outlining her cheek. In spite of herself she trembled at that touch. "It seems we've got a lot to learn about each other, and there's not much time, partner."

The word was spoken lightly but it snapped her out of her dazed, unaccountable response. A rush of indignation countered the effect of his nearness. Of course it had all been another ploy, a calculated manipulation to break down her defenses and get her to agree to what he wanted. He'd told her he liked a challenge, and no doubt refusal by a woman was the kind of challenge that someone like Griff Deane most enjoyed.

"No, we're not partners," she said. Her voice was small at first but grew stronger as she added, "I think you'd better go, Griff. It's a long drive back to Tilikit, and if you're really serious about getting out on the trail with me, five o'clock comes awfully fast." She did not wait for his reaction but walked swiftly toward the solid safety of her spruce-log cabin.

She did not see the expression on his face, the determination that curled his lips into a small smile. Her coolness didn't fool him. He had felt her swift response to his kiss, and while it had shaken him, it had also strengthened his resolve. Griff Deane never went after anything he wanted without getting it, and he wanted this woman as his partner. His smile widened, and his clear voice checked her at the door of her cabin.

"Sleep well, Beth. Remember, I've got a whole week to change your mind."

Chapter Three

There was a stiff wind blowing outside, and it curled its cold fingers through Bethany's long hair when she opened the door for Griff early next morning. His lean cheeks were ruddy with cold, but the expression in those green eyes brought the remembered warmth of last night.

"Good morning, Beth." For a moment, his deep voice stressed the familiar contraction of her name. "Am I late?"

"Five minutes early, in point of fact." She gave him a cool, unconcerned little smile which was a lie. His height and the breadth of his shoulders in the lamp-lit warmth of her cabin were disturbing. Lamp glow and light thrown by the wood stove caught his tall, rugged silhouette and lengthened it against the rough wood wall, creating an illusion of enormous power.

"It's very nice in here." He was smiling as he took in the wall hangings and bookcases, the battery powered radio and record player, handmade furniture and bright cushions that decorated the low, wide couch that doubled as her bed. Was he mentally contrasting this one-room cabin with its neat little cooking area to some plush town house in New York? No doubt.

"Someday I'm going to get hold of a generator that will bring electricity to the cabin," she told him.

"Meanwhile, I have the lamps and my batteries and a great source of water." He looked a question, and she started to pull on her parka. "I was just going to get my daily supply."

"Do you want company?"

About to refuse help, she found herself nodding. Perhaps it would do the great corporation president good to see what wilderness living was all about.

"Why not? The lake from which I draw my water is about half a mile from the cabin." She handed him a flashlight and drew on her parka and gloves. "I warn you, it's a cold walk."

He made no comment as he followed her outside, hefting the two large metal buckets outside the cabin door. "You know your way well," he said, as they followed the beam of her flashlight through the dark that surrounded the cabin. "Is there a path to the lake?"

She shook her head. "I've tried not to make paths or clear the grounds near my cabin. I didn't want to interfere with nature any more than I had to."

When they reached the lake, she showed him where she always cut a hole through the thick ice. "This way I only have to contend with an icy crust instead of a whole layer of ice," she explained as she dipped her pails into the water.

"Let me." He took the pails from her and filled them with a practiced ease. He also insisted on carrying both buckets back to the cabin. "Now that that's done," he then said, "do we begin our training, partner?"

She ignored the last word. "I've already fed the dogs and they're raring to go. I've brought some snacks for both our teams, also. All we need to do is harness our sleds."

Griff had brought his sled on the back of his snowmobile. As he greeted his new team and harnessed them, Bethany had to admire his deft handling of both dogs and equipment. She had intended to go only short distances today, but watching him made her change her mind. "We'll travel about sixty miles today," she told him. "Our teams will have to go longer distances before they can run in the Rohn Relay."

"You're the boss, Beth." Again his voice deepened on her name, and she hastily concentrated on what she was doing. The air was cold and dry, and the dogs' breath was freezing on their muzzles as she snapped on the toggles and harnessed them. Last night was a mistake and best forgotten, she told herself. It would have to be forgotten or she could never endure a week with this man.

As she finished her preparations, she became aware that Griff had already completed his harnessing and was waiting for her. "Ready?" he asked, and she caught the note of intense eagerness and enjoyment that she had heard in his voice last night when he spoke of success.

She flicked her reins. "Gee, Katiktok—right!" she commanded, and they were on their way.

It was a long, sometimes unnerving day. Several times during the hours of racing and instruction, Bethany found herself alternating between surprise at Griff's ability and pleasure in the teamwork he already exhibited. If it had been anyone else, instructing him would have been pure joy. Griff's natural quickness and instincts more than made up for his lack of experience. Besides, she quickly saw, he had a good eye and a quick ear and a respect for his dogs.

She could and did teach him several things, including tips about the weather. Most cheechakos, she told him, were under the impression that Alaska was constantly snow-covered and prey to sudden storms. "Old sourdoughs like me know that's not so. The part of Alaska in which I live does well to get a foot of snow a year, and the weather usually stays steady for days. There might be seven days of clear, dry weather and a ten-day period of storms."

He listened carefully to what she said, but smiled at the end. "I doubt if you can be described as a sour-dough, Beth. A delectable croissant, perhaps . . ."

Hurriedly, she broke in to make another observation. They had come to a twenty-mile checkpoint, and she told him that it was time he switched the positioning of the dogs.

"Your strongest pair is Pancho and Lexi," she pointed out. "They need to be closest to your sled. And isn't Victorine slacking off?"

"I suspected she was, but I didn't know for sure. How can you tell?" When she explained that a dog's weariness or hurt or laziness could be seen from the way it held its head or tail or ears, he laughed. "You make it sound so easy, Beth. I thought it was ESP." He paused and added thoughtfully, "I see that it's possible to read dogs' body language as well as people's. I can— Good Lord, what is that?"

An odd, clicking sound had been coming across the thin layer of snow, and now a cumbersome shape appeared through a clump of spruce and fir. Huge, heavy-antlered, its head lowered indecisively, a great bull moose stared moodily at humans and dogs.

The dogs had started to bark wildly. Aladin and Growler as well as Griff's big males began to hurl themselves forward against their gang line. As Bethany struggled to control her team, she saw Griff pull himself and his sled in front of her, forming a barrier between her and the big animal.

"Will it attack?" he asked quietly.

As he spoke, the big beast turned its heavy head and began to move away, its ankle bones creating the

odd clicking rhythm they had heard before. Bethany
drew a deep breath. "They're unpredictable. Sometimes they'll ignore you and sometimes . . ." her
voice trailed off. "I've heard of mushers whose teams
have been mangled by moose when they charged
right at the sled." She frowned as Griff turned his
sled and dogs. "It wasn't necessary for you to put
yourself and your dogs in my path. I really can take
care of myself, Griff. I've been doing so for years."

"Ah, but I wasn't nearby then." His smile flashed
at her, as he added, "So that was our excitement for
the day. Do we go on or stop for a while and rest the
dogs?"

She decided to call a halt. While the dogs were
chewing their snacks of honey balls—meatballs made
of ground beef, honey vegetable oil, and vitamins—
she returned to the subject of the moose.

"You're inexperienced in Alaskan racing, Griff.
Moose are only a very occasional hazard. It's the terrain along the Rohn Relay that will be difficult.
There's a place called Rainy Pass, for instance. It's
between Settlers Bay and Rohn, and there are enormous boulders that just seem to jump out at you as
you drive by. The whole pass is only a couple of feet
wide, and it twists and turns on a steep cliff over the
Dalveell Gorge. One slip could mean your death."

He smiled. "I enjoy a challenge but I don't go in for
being foolhardy," he told her. "I've skied and done a
great deal of mountain climbing, Bethany. You
needn't be concerned that I'd endanger myself or the
dogs in such dangerous places as Rainy Pass any
more than you would."

Of course the idea of danger wouldn't phase him,
she thought. "Skiing and mountain climbing are soli-
tary sports," she said. "Is there a reason you chose
them?"

He shrugged. "Corporate management taught me

many things. One of them was that, in the last analy-
sis, I can only depend on myself. That's true in sports
and business as well. Which is why, though I have
excellent people working for me at Deane, I make the
final decisions."

There spoke the big business mogul again. "I'm
surprised you are actually taking a partner this
time," she said, and he grinned at the tartness in her
voice.

"Just for the Rohn Relay, Beth. And the Rohn event
is just a means to an end. I intend to win the Iditarod
in March, you see."

She said crisply, "You'll have to beat a lot of seasoned competition, Griff. Including me."

"It would be a pleasure to challenge you," he said,
and she knew he meant it. Looking into the lean,
smiling face, she suddenly realized why he wanted
to be partnered by "the best." He wants to learn
everything I can do and then beat me with my own
skills, she thought. Instead of angering her, the
knowledge made her smile. Well, she would teach
him—and she would best *him*. Two could most certainly play at a game.

"Does that smile mean that you're contemplating
becoming my partner?" he was asking. She laughed
and got to her feet.

"Certainly the corporate world has taught you the
value of suspense, Mr. Deane," she joked. "I have a
week to make up my mind—remember? Meanwhile,
we'd better get started before the dogs give up on us."

The rest of the morning and most of the afternoon
were spent both in racing for speed and in practical
lessons. Bethany showed Griff how to make position
changes among the dogs during a race. "In a race the
speed with which you can switch dogs may mean the
difference between winning and losing," she
explained. She also began to show him some differ-

ent techniques of racing, but soon stopped doing so.
Griff, she saw, had his own distinctive style. He
leaned far over his sled, giving his dogs a slightly different center of gravity, a little less weight to pull.
Although most of her dogs could easily pull at a rate
of 18 to 20 miles per hour, she saw that Griff's
method might easily shave more minutes off his
time.

By the time they returned to her cabin, it was late
in the afternoon. Dogs and riders were somewhat
weary but happy with the day's workout. "It's an
unwritten law that mushers have to take care of their
dogs first," Bethany explained to Griff as he helped
her put fish meal, meat, beef tallow, and vitamins
into a kettle for a nourishing stew. Griff held his nose
over the terrible smell, and she said, "I know you
won't believe this, but it's good for them."

"I'll take your word for it. I was hungry when you
started cooking this brew, but I'm not so sure now,"
he countered, laughing.

Bethany stopped in the act of tipping the stew into
dog bowls and looked at him. She herself was raven-
ous. It had been a wearying day, and she had been
thinking longingly of the sauna she had built onto the
cabin in lieu of a modern bath or shower. But as she
watched Griff feed his dogs, lovingly and carefully
inspecting their feet and rubbing their ears in praise,
something within her moved. He must be tired, too,
she thought. He must be just as hungry as I am.

She spoke almost without thinking, certainly without reasoning. "I've got some frozen moose steaks in
the woodshed," she said. "If you're willing to try
them, there's more than enough for two."

"It's the best offer I've had today. That is, if fried
moose steak doesn't smell like this stuff. I also pre-
sume that your moose's no kin to that character we
met on the trail today," was Griff's light rejoinder,

and the hesitation in Bethany fell away. Last night had been forgotten in the camaraderie which they had achieved on the trail today. Tonight they were mushers together, and they would share a meal and talk about the day and go their separate ways.

He brought in armfuls of wood for the stove while she sawed off pieces of moose and fried it together with canned corn, beans, and sourdough pancakes. They washed their faces and hands companionably in the plastic bucket beside the kitchen area, and while they set the table spoke of various dogs and difficulties encountered in the day's training. They were not exactly friends, Bethany thought, but the tension of yesterday had dissipated. I'm glad I asked him to stay, she thought. I'm not sure whether he's going to end up my partner or my rival out there in the race, but I've got to get to know him better either way.

They were starving by the time they sat down to eat, and food had never tasted so good. Bethany joyfully ate her way through three helpings of steak and vegetables, and finished by mopping up the last of the pan juices with a hunk of sourdough bread. As she was popping it into her mouth, she looked up and saw Griff leaning back in his chair watching her.

"I've never seen a woman enjoy her food as much," he said with a grin. "Most of the people I know are either on a diet or too tense to eat." He paused, and his green eyes moved appreciatively over her high breasts and slender waist. "What's more, on you the food seems to know where to go. At least it fills out just the right places."

He reached across the rough wooden table and took her hand in his. As his fingers touched hers it was back—instantly and with greater impact than ever before. Bethany felt her heart jolt with the strange, the irresistible tension that had been present from their first meeting.

She pulled her hand away, but he had felt it too, and was almost as disturbed as she. He hadn't meant anything but a light compliment, a friendly remark toward a lovely, gutsy woman. But he had known beautiful women before, had been excited and intrigued by them. He had had many women, respecting most and caring for many even when the physical love that had bound him to them dissolved. But he had never once felt this odd, inexplicable pull which made his senses come to pulsing life. Griff had to battle with himself to keep from drawing her into his arms, for that would be a tactical error. Even knowing Bethany as little as he did, he knew he could not win her partnership this way.

She broke the tension abruptly by getting up and walking toward the wood stove. She sank down on the couch and tried to get her heartbeat back to normal. Why did she have to feel so nervous? It had been just a touch. That, and the look in his green eyes. Suddenly she felt a restless, aching hunger within her, as keen as the low moan of the wind outside.

"What's the matter? It's just the wind." He had seen her shiver, and he tried to smile easily at her as he came to stand before her with his back to the wood stove.

She jumped at the chance to change the subject. "Julie always told me that Talka's spirit was in the wind, calling for Nonak."

"Talka—the woman racer that gave her name to Lover's Run," he said. "Julie didn't say much about the legend last night, but I suspect a sad story. Legends usually tell of thwarted love or star-crossed lovers."

"It is sad, in a way . . ." He came over and pulled a cushion from the couch, sat down at her feet, and looked up into her face as she spoke. She was intensely aware of his closeness, her senses acutely alert to the unique fragrance of faint aftershave and fresh outdoors that emanated from him. If she reached out, her fingers could touch the crisp dark hair that shaded his forehead. "Talka and Nonak were Eskimos. They were both brave hunters and expert sled runners, and they were lovers. Julie says that they were both beautiful."

He smiled and reached out to brush back a strand of her red-gold hair. "All lovers are beautiful to each other," he said.

She wanted to pull away from his touch and at the same time she wanted to lean closer. To mask her confusion she continued. "Talka lived in Anvik. She was the only child of a famous hunter there, and the old man brought her up as a son. She bested all the young swains that came around courting, and she let it be known she wasn't going to marry anybody but a real man. Naturally, Nonak, who lived near Tilikit, heard of her. He went to Anvik, courted her, and they fell in love."

"Did he outdo her on the hunt?" Griff asked, his green eyes interested.

"I don't know. All I know is that they came to live out here until an outbreak of diphtheria raced through Anvik. The lovers were asked to take serum to the people in Anvik, and in spite of bad weather they started out. They made Anvik all right, but on the way home the weather got terrible. They were separated, and Nonak was lost in the storm. Talka could have made it home, but she didn't. She looked for Nonak and when she found him, he was dead, frozen. Next morning, rescuers found both of them together."

"She could have saved herself. She should have,"

Griff said. "What good did her death do him? If he loved her, he'd have wanted her safe."

Bethany shook her head. "You don't understand. In the wilderness, you learn to depend on each other. You have to. Talka could no more go off and leave Nonak than she could fly." She paused. "Anyway, Julie always ended the story happily. She said that both the lovers are now happy together in the Kingdom of the Polar Star."

He smiled. "I wonder what kind of kingdom that is? It sounds cold and bleak, but I suppose it wouldn't seem like that to Talka and Nonak. They would have each other to hold in the long dark nights under the northern lights." His deep voice was thoughtful, almost tender. And then he said, "Beth. Bethany—"

Had he moved? Had she? Was that how it came about that their arms were around each other? He was kneeling on the floor before her, and she was no longer seated on the couch but kneeling also within the perimeter of his arms. She could feel the hardness of his chest, the wild beat of his heart answering her. In the tumult of her senses, she tipped back her face to look up at him and saw the intensity of his emerald eyes.

"Griff—" She had intended it as a protest, but the sound was smothered against his mouth. His lips were warm, remembered. The clamor of her senses that had begun yesterday brought each sense to yearning wakefulness. He whispered her name as he caressed her mouth with his lips, his tongue, brushing, touching, sipping the satin honey of her.

Sensations that she hadn't been aware could exist in her work-tired body imploded within her. She felt the warm heaviness of her breasts, the ready tenderness of her nipples against the flannel shirt she wore. She felt an urge to move closer, seek deeper kisses, and as if intuiting her desire, he held her closer. One large hand spread against the straightness of her back, the other made a cradle for her suddenly heavy head. A curtain of her red-gold hair rippled back over his hand and arm, a cascade of fiery silk that rippled and moved as she pressed against him.

Was he murmuring her name? She could not distinguish the separate words, but the deep, many-shaded voice was stroking and caressing and kissing her as well as his mouth. And now his hand was moving, rubbing the line of her back, curving across her rib cage and pulling the shirt from the waistband of her ski pants. His hand was as sensitive as his mouth as it curved around her rounded breasts, delicately traced sensual patterns against her soft, wanting flesh, circling but not yet touching the tautness of her nipples. She wanted him to touch her. She moved impatiently against him, and then gasped as loving fingers found the tightly furled buds.

Outside, the wind was rising, and one of the dogs banged his feeding tin. Loud barking resulted. She heard the familiar sound as if from very far away, heard it as a distant sea against her consciousness. Her reality, her world was Griff's arms around her, and now his fingers undoing the buttons of her shirt. His mouth left hers to trace a line of incandescent fire from throat to the inner curve of her breast. His mouth teased her, denying the wanting thrust of her nipples.

"Oh, Griff," she sighed, and he murmured some word deep in his throat as his warm mouth closed around the yearning flower of her breast. She felt the tug of his lips and the butterfly-light touch of his tongue and then the rub of his cheek against her smooth skin, a movement that was part caress, part male roughness, male demand.

Already he was tugging down the waistband of her

ski pants. She could not resist, did not want to resist this. In a moment, she knew, she would be naked in his arms; and she wanted desperately to be naked, free from the barrier of cloth, and the other, more difficult barriers between them.

She did not want to think of them, but already those barriers were forming in her mind. And as the thoughts came, the white liquid heat that was coursing through her veins and through every nerve end of her body slowly cooled. She must not—could not—not with Griff Deane!

She moved, pulling away from his magical hands and his drugging kisses, shifting so that she was no longer pressed against him. She put both her palms on his powerful chest, dimly realizing that at some point his shirt, too, had been unbuttoned and she could feel the smooth-muscled flesh against her palms. "No," she whispered. "We mustn't do this."

He did not let her go. "Why not?" he asked her, and his voice was deeper than she had yet heard it, vibrant with the same sensual flames that had licked and darted through her. "We're both adults. I want you, and you want me to make love to you. After today, it's natural . . ."

She cut into his words. "*Because* of today we mustn't," she said almost desperately. "Don't you see? We worked hard together today and we felt—we felt a kind of camaraderie. It's natural. People who work together on the trail often feel it. But we can't mistake it for—we mustn't let it get away from us." She realized that he still held her, saw the intensity in those remarkable eyes and whispered, "We can't. Not if we want to win this Rohn Relay. Business can't mix with pleasure."

His eyebrows raised, and some of the intensity changed in his lean face. Lamplight traced the curve of a smile on his lips. "You mean that as partners we can't let sexual attraction interfere with what we do on the trail?"

"I don't know. I didn't mean that to sound as a commitment, but if we ever did decide to become partners, we couldn't allow personal involvement," she said. This time there was no doubt about it. She *was* desperate. She knew that if he negated her words, if he pulled her back against that solid wall of his strength, she would go. Forgetting everything, she would melt against him, meld with him.

But he did not draw her close. Instead, she felt his arms loosen, his hands let go. But not altogether. His hands went to cradle her face in a strangely gentle caress. "All right," he said, and she wondered how quickly his voice could return to normal. "That makes sense. Until we make some decision on our partnership, there'll be no more of this."

She pulled on her shirt with shaking fingers and watched him rise to his height with a powerfully graceful movement. "I'll be here tomorrow at five to help you get the water from the lake," he said. Then, he bent down and lifted her to her feet. For a fleeting moment, dark, troubled eyes met green, and it seemed to her that he frowned, more in puzzlement than in irritation.

"Good night," she said hesitantly, and was relieved when he stepped away. Then, wordlessly, he took one of her hands and lifted it, kissed the palm, and folded her fingers around the imprint of his lips. And left her.

Chapter Four

~❧~

The kiss on her palm did not burn. It gave off a slow, measured heat that pulsed as if she were cradling a coal whose heart still glowed with fire. In an unconscious gesture she opened her fist and rubbed the palm against her cheek. As she did so, she remembered the warmth of Griff's lean body against hers, the way he had stroked and kissed and caressed her. When memory touched the moment when his mouth had closed over her eager nipples, she shivered, and a wash of desire sighed through her.

"Enough of this," she said out loud as if Griff were there to hear her. Impatiently, she bundled into outdoor clothes and pulled on boots to go and check the dogs. She desperately needed some everyday chore to pull normalcy back into her shaken world.

Outside the cabin she was assailed by howling wind. She stood still and adjusted to it while looking up at the sky. The night was clear and the bright stars seemed close enough to touch. Glittering scarves of the northern lights brought out shades of white and deep indigo in the cabin and its surroundings. When the wind dropped, she could scent woodsmoke and the piny tang of spruce.

"I love this place; I want no other kind of life." Bethany wondered why she even bothered to articulate such a thought. She was solidly and completely content—or had been until yesterday. And really, nothing had changed since yesterday. Her dogs, her cabin, her independence, and the great challenge of the outdoors were what she wanted and would always love.

"And I wouldn't jeopardize any of it for a man, certainly not for Griff," she told Katiktok. "It's crazy even thinking that his coming here makes a difference in how I think or live. He's here to have a thrill racing the Rohn Relay—period. His thrills aren't going to include getting chummy with me."

She spent a long time outside and later relaxed in the small sauna that was attached to the cabin and could be reached through a door in the cabin wall. Though the rest of her one-room cabin had been a joint effort with Piers, this primitive sauna was the work of her own hands. Now she sat in the small, dark, sod-roofed hut and dashed water on rocks heated to a red glow inside the sauna's big wood stove. Usually, the cleansing sweat and then the invigorating wash in cool lake water relaxed her completely, but tonight she was too conscious of her body. Her high, firm breasts seemed swollen, her nipples tender. Her resolution not to allow any further closeness with Griff didn't help, either, and she clenched her hands, still feeling his kiss. If he even hints at getting friendly again, I'll break our agreement, she thought.

To her relief, Griff seemed inclined to follow her line of thought. For the next few days, their relationship was on a purely professional level. He seemed more concerned with the weather—which forecasts said was due to change within the week and turn stormy—than with romance, and when they were out running their teams, his attitude was strictly business. He continued to learn quickly and more than once used his new knowledge and his strength to good advantage on the track. What was more, he cooperated with her fully, showing himself to be an excellent partner.

And yet Bethany held back from making the final commitment. Certainly, there weren't many men as skillful or as strong as Griff. If it were anybody else, she kept thinking each night after he had seen to his team, wished her good night at her cabin door, and roared off to Tilikit on his snowmobile. If he were simply another musher, not a man whose watchful green eyes could still make her pulses leap. Griff Deane was behaving himself, but Bethany distrusted the look in those eyes.

Julie Kobuk couldn't understand why Bethany was dragging her feet. She rode out to Lover's Run and the cabin late one afternoon on Elmer's old snowmobile which, she said, had stalled out twice on the way from Tilikit.

"Dumb machines," she said feelingly. "I always liked dogs better. Griff said the same thing when he helped me fix this old contraption so I could come visit you." She paused. "Thought I'd bring some fish over to you. Weather's going to turn bad soon, they're saying."

Bethany nodded and welcomed Julie into her cabin. "I figure the storm will hit late tomorrow or maybe day after next."

"Good thing it didn't come before." Julie paused meaningfully. "You've made up your mind about going partners with Griff, haven't you?"

Bethany didn't answer. "I'm not sure," she finally said. "He's an excellent driver, but I don't think we'd be good as partners." Julie snorted and Bethany added, "No, it's true. We're both too competitive for one thing. Griff told me that someday he's going to beat me out on the race trail."

"And what's the harm in a little competition?" Julie stuck out an aggressive chin. "You always were too independent and stubborn for your own good, Bethany Sheridan. About time a man like Griff came by who can stand up to you."

There was a subtle note in Julie's scolding, and Bethany raised her eyebrows. "You wouldn't be trying to set me up, Julie?" she asked. "If you are, it won't work."

"And why not? It's been awhile since Piers. I know that didn't work out, but men and women aren't supposed to live solo. They need partners." Bethany shook her head. "Why not Griff? He's a good man."

"Maybe so." She spoke slowly, letting her thoughts take form not only for Julie but for herself. "Griff and I belong to different worlds, Julie. He loves challenge and power just for the sake of thrills. I enjoy this kind of life, and racing, too, for the pure joy of it. To me, winning is a way of raising money to keep living the kind of life I love. To Griff, it's just another thrill . . ."

"And you don't find him the slightest bit attractive?" Julie hinted.

Bethany hesitated, then answered as honestly as she dared. "He's an attractive man—but what I need is a partner I can depend on, not some thrill-seeking business mogul. Griff represents things I dislike, Julie. I don't think he means badly, but he can't help manipulating people to get what he wants. And he's rich and used to having people cater to him. No. He's not the partner for me."

She had finally made her decision, but the relief she had been sure would come with the decision eluded her. "How will you tell Griff?" Julie asked, and again Bethany hesitated.

"Tomorrow," she finally said. "It's going to storm, and we won't be going out in the bad weather, anyway. He can look around for another partner. Didn't I hear from someone that Ben Mihailouk is looking for a partner for the Rohn?"

She fully intended to tell Griff first thing next morning, but for some reason she kept putting off her decision. It wasn't until they stopped at midpoint after a long forty-mile run that she finally broached the subject.

"Julie came by the cabin yesterday," she began.

"I know. I helped put that snowmobile of Elmer's together again. I also offered to drive her to your cabin, but she knew that the plane was waiting for me and didn't want to hold me up." Her eyebrows rose in mute question, and he explained that radio messages and an unsatisfactory phone link hadn't been enough. "I've arranged for a private plane to bring mail and documents from Anchorage to Raedar every few days. It's necessary that I keep a line open to New York, and this seemed the most painless way."

The cost of having a plane come by so often must be prodigious. She shook her head at the thought, realizing that this was just another indication of the difference between their worlds. "Griff," she said, hesitating no longer, "you've learned as much as I can teach. From now on I feel you can be on your own."

"Is this some sort of graduation?" Though his words were humorous, there was an edge to his voice, and she knew he had understood what she really meant.

"We agreed on a week's trial," she pointed out. "I don't think a partnership between us would work, that's all."

"May I ask why?" He wasn't used to being refused so casually, but Griff knew there was more to it. He felt disappointment and quick anger, which he reined in tightly. Bethany, he saw, wasn't happy with the decision herself.

"We're too competitive," she was saying.

Shaking his head he said, "That's an excuse. You know that I can be a cooperative and intuitive partner. What's your real reason, Bethany? Are you afraid of me?"

"Afraid of you!" she exploded. "Don't flatter yourself." For a moment she glared at him, then she stalked to her sled, pulled on the lines. She called out to Katiktok and started her team without looking back to see whether Griff was following.

She soon realized that he was following. She heard his low, tense "*Haw*, Lexi!" as his sled moved to the left, and then drew alongside her. They were both traveling at a good speed, but his team was gaining on her. Angrily, Bethany shouted to her own dogs. He was going to beat her, was he? They'd see about that!

Back over the terrain they hurtled, and Bethany was so engrossed in her own private duel that she did not realize the change in the sky. Before they had gone halfway the distance home, the wind had increased tremendously, and the sky had darkened. Snow, hurled along by the strong gusts of wind, buffeted them.

For a moment she considered calling a halt to the angry race. If she dropped back and stopped, she had no doubt that he, too, would stop. But he was moving ahead of her, moving quickly, too. She could not give up without showing weakness. Besides, she thought grimly, the Rohn Relay and the Iditarod would be driven through storms far greater than this one. Without losing an instant of speed, she snapped a headlamp over her forehead and turned on the beam. In front of her, Griff had done exactly the same.

It was then that she saw that one of her dogs was

beginning to limp. Young Aladin was favoring his left hind foot. In a real race she might let him see whether he could work out what might be a cramp. As it was, she halted her team with difficulty and pulled him out of the line, lifting his paw to examine it. As she had feared, the paw was red and tender-looking. She was lifting Aladin into the sled when she realized that Griff had stopped his team.

"Are you all right?" he shouted against the growing roar of the storm.

"Yes! Go on—I'll follow!" she called. And then, she saw what was happening. The hooked "anchor" with which she kept her sled stable and at rest had pulled free of the snow. As she placed Aladin in the sled, he wriggled out of her arms and barked excitedly, setting his teammates into action. Before her horrified eyes she saw the team and sled take off without her.

She had no time to think, no time to start in pursuit, before she saw Griff's sled pull up close to her. He hauled her in beside him and, without a word, began to forge ahead in pursuit of the runaway team. It was not an easy race. Burdened with her weight as well as Griff's, the dogs were not as swift as Bethany's team. Joyously, Katiktok led her mates off the usual track and into wide fields that were now swirling with windblown snow.

They caught up to the team near an icy slope where the dogs paused and finally stopped. "Wait here," Griff told Bethany, tossing her the lines. Mortified, she made no protest as he strode over to her runaway team. But as she watched, she cried out a warning. Griff's tall form slipped, then slid backward on the treacherous ice.

"Are you hurt?" she yelled against the wind.

"No—all right!" His voice sounded odd, even against the backdrop of the storm. He was probably furious at her, and rightly so. Tiredly, Bethany tried to point out to herself that this wasn't the first time that an experienced musher lost her team and had overexcited dogs run away from her. Griff would not see what had happened in such a light.

His behavior when he brought back her team made this abundantly clear. "Can you handle them now?" was all he asked, but there was a cold, disgusted undertone to his voice that both angered and hurt her.

"Yes. Thank you for your help. It happens sometimes that—"

"Must we stay out in the storm and discuss it?" he demanded. "We'd better find our way back to the track. Do you want to lead, or shall I?"

The storm had picked up even more strength, and she knew that he was right. It was foolish not to try and get to shelter as soon as possible. Still, as she led the last fifteen miles to the cabin, Bethany felt indignation curl and uncurl within her. If this was the way Griff was going to act, she was grateful that she had quashed any possibility of a partnership between them. And yet, she thought, he came back for me. He stopped and came back when he felt I was in trouble and needed his help.

The outline of the cabin had never looked so solid or as welcome as it did now through whirling snow and wind. She turned to Griff to tell him this, and saw with a sudden jab of fear that he was not standing in his sled but had affected an odd, slumped-over position. "Griff!" she exclaimed. "Are you all right?"

Had he been hurt after all when he fell on the ice? Her heart thudding when he didn't answer, she jumped out of her sled and ran across the snow to him. When her headlamp shone on his face, she cried out. His face looked blue with cold.

"Griff!" she shouted, and his mouth twisted into a ghost of a smile.

"I'm all right. A bit cold. Fell in the water back there—" His teeth were chattering so badly he could hardly say the words.

Water! Bethany herself felt as if she'd stepped through a hole in the ice. Water, if allowed to soak right through a person's clothes, could freeze and induce hypothermia. She shook Griff as hard as she could. "Get in the cabin," she said. "Get into the cabin right now!"

"The dogs. Remember, a musher's unwritten law is . . ."

"I'll get the dogs later. First I have to take care of you. Don't stand there and try and be a hero, Griff Deane. Get into the cabin!" she cried.

She pushed him into the dark cabin and made him get as close to the stove as possible. "Take off your clothes," she ordered. "Strip off everything."

"What!"

"You can freeze on your own time, not on mine." She was already tearing at his outer garments, horrified to find them frozen into stiff ice. His sweater was no better, nor his shirt and undershirt. She pulled them from him unceremoniously, then carried all the blankets from her bed and covered his shaking torso with them. "Take your ski pants and your long johns off, too. And your socks. Hurry!"

"I hear and obey." Even at such a time, there was amusement in his deep tones, but she didn't pay any attention to him. Still in her outer clothes, she rushed into the sauna and began to heat the wood stove, shoving seasoned wood deep into its heart and placing the steam stones in as well. Hurry and warm up, she begged the rocks. She knew that in spite of his bravado, Griff was thoroughly chilled.

She realized just how chilled when she returned

and found him shivering by the stove. "Can't seem to—get warm. I've been a lot wetter but never c-c-c-colder," he commented, between chattering teeth.

She stripped off her parka and warmed her hands at the stove, and then began to massage his back and chest and arms with her hands. Gooseflesh stood out sharp against her hands as she rubbed at him, trying to get his circulation going. "It'll be all right." She had completely forgotten their argument, her decision, even who this was. He was just some frozen musher, a comrade of the trails, and she was going to take care of him. "I've got the sauna started and it'll soon be very warm in there. The warm steam will help. You'll be all right."

He said nothing, but she could feel the great muscles of his arms and shoulders ripple against her ministering hands. He was still so cold!

"A stupid thing to do, trying to race you with the storm coming on," he said, his deep voice raw with the shivers he was trying to surpress. "Trying to be macho—angry at you. I'm sorry, Beth."

He moved, and under the rough blankets the hard nakedness of muscle-hard buttocks and long, sinewy line of thigh pressed against her for a moment. At any other time her senses would have reacted in complete confusion at this nearness. Now, she was only afraid for him.

"Let's get you to the sauna, Griff. Keep one of the blankets around you."

Luckily, the small hut was already quite warm, and when she splashed the heated stones with water, comforting steam rose in great clouds. She took a rough towel and exposing his torso, began to rub hard against his back and chest. As she worked, steam and sweat ran down her face and arms and back, until in impatience she pulled off her sweater and woolen undervest, her sodden ski pants, and worked in more comfortable near nakedness. He couldn't see her in the dark hut, anyway.

After some time she felt a change in him. He was still cold but no longer icy, and his voice no longer as strained. "How do you feel?" she asked.

"Better." Ruefully, he admitted, "I've had massages before but never like this. I have a feeling you rescued me from freezing to death, Beth."

Something in his voice and in the way he spoke her name made her skin warm even more. Though it was dark, she wrapped the towel she had been using around her and backed a little distance from him. As she did so, she saw a small light glow on and realized that he'd snapped on her headlamp. She hadn't even realized she'd brought it with her when she hurried him into the sauna.

"So this is your sauna." He was looking around appreciatively. There were wooden benches near the stove, and he went to sit down on one of them, the blanket now wrapped loosely around his loins and hips. "I've never been more glad to see a sauna. What happened to me out there, Beth?"

"I'm not sure, but my guess is that you stepped on an overflow. Out here streams and rivers can freeze up suddenly. Free-flowing water sometimes gets dammed up just under the surface of new ice. The water hasn't got any place to go, so it sort of backs up and accumulates and gathers pressure until it finds a weak spot in the ice. Then, it bursts right through over the ice top."

"And turns to brittle ice so that a cheechako like me can put his big feet in it," Griff said ruefully. He reached out to splash more water on the stones, and she saw his muscles move like silk under his skin. She had worked on him so closely, so intimately, and now the memory embarrassed her. She closed her eyes against the remembered feel of his body under her hands pressed close against hers, and leaned back.

"You look comfortable." He leaned back in the semidark and watched her with surprise and pleasure. He had thought her beautiful before, but now the light of the headlamp turned her fair skin luminous, etched in red and gold and pearl against the dark. He watched the rise and fall of the towel that covered her rounded breasts, raised his eyes to trace the eyelids, closed and shell-pink, the rosy mouth that somehow now gave an aura of fragile vulnerability.

Bethany, fragile? She had more than likely saved his life just now. Yet, he was conscious of a shift within himself, a great welling of tenderness that was almost like pain. It scared him as the prospect of death hadn't done, and he moved restlessly.

The sound of his shifting made her open her eyes. She started to ask him if he was feeling warm, now, and stopped. The look in those green eyes, intense through the clouds of white steam, stopped her. He was no longer a frozen comrade but Griff, and she was suddenly not so much frightened as very aware. Under the rough towel she felt her breasts swell, the nipples tautening against the coarse fabric as they remembered the roughness and demand of his cheek, his lips.

"I think I'd better look after the dogs," she said, but could not gather the energy to stand while he looked at her like that. "You stay and enjoy the sauna."

"I hadn't expected you to possess such a luxury," he said, knowing that she was prepared to run, wanting her to stay. Wanting her. Or was the feeling that shadowed his mind and body simply want? "Did you think of this yourself?"

"It's not an original idea. Many Indian villages have their communal bathhouses with a plank

in-between so that the sexes can be segregated."
Now, decidedly, she got to her feet.

"Bethany."

He had risen at the same moment, so that they
stood facing each other across the steaming stones.
There was a moment when the world seemed to hush
and stand still. Bethany was aware of the beat of her
own pulse, the sound of steam, and the sigh of their
breathing.

Slowly, almost reverently, he reached out and
touched her hair, pushing it gently back behind her
ears. "I haven't thanked you yet, have I?" he said.

"No need. I told you that people have to depend on
each other in the wilderness . . ." She tried to speak
evenly, but her words trailed away as his hands on
her bare shoulders stopped her.

Before she could think or draw breath, he had
drawn her into the circle of his arms. She gasped at
the shock of bare flesh against bare flesh—the soft
silken swell above her towel melding with the furred
hardness of his chest. Then, his mouth had come
down on hers, slow and sensuous and knowing every
nuance of her lips. At her back, his hands moved
knowingly, purposefully, unfastening the brief towel
that covered her, lightly smoothing the line of her
back, over her still-clothed hips, her bare thighs.

She sighed in acknowledgment of the flame that
was sweeping through her. In soundless answer,
there was more sensation: a hardness, alien but welcome, as his thigh pressed boldly between her legs
while one strong hand flattened against her hips and
lifted her toward him. Against him. She could feel
her body's movement, feel her captive hips strain forward, draw away in a rhythm as primitive as the wild
drumbeat of her heart.

His mouth left hers and moved to her throat,
tongue, and lips, leaving an imprint of drugging fire.

Then, without disturbing the line of toweling still covering her breasts, he lowered his mouth along the beginning slope of her breasts. His open-mouthed kisses made some secret, deep place within her contract in joy and then seek release in small, sensuous shivers. He reacted, closing his mouth first around one yearning nipple, then the other.

She caught his head against her, fingers curling and stroking the dark, crisp hair as she had often yearned to do. His hair was moist from the damp mist that swirled around them both, and his mouth was warm also, suckling gently but insistently. She needed to touch him, hold him closer, and her hands moved urgently down the strong shoulders and back, over the lean line of his back, and over his firm buttocks.

She realized that his covering blanket had fallen to the floor also, and for a long moment she felt the power of him, the musculature of chest and belly and thigh and the demand of his male deisre. For that moment she pressed against him, held him against her, and then he moved. The small movement emphasized his want of her. She felt his hands go down, the thumbs slide under the fragile fabric of her last garment. In a moment it would be gone, the last fragile barrier between them. For a moment she tensed, and then felt the surge of that tension break like a high, cresting wave against the hardness of his enfolding arms. She could no longer fight free of the truth. She wanted Griff, had always wanted him.

"Beth?" She opened her eyes, dark eyelashes fluttering up over eyes that answered his question before he asked it. She thought that he would sweep her into his arms but instead he stood there, his hold on hers lessening just enough so that she could lean back in his arms. As she did so, a shriek of wind dinned against the wall of the sauna, and a tendril of cold curled into the room from some not entirely windproofed point.

"Are you cold?" he murmured, his voice husky and soft. She had not heard him use that voice before. "Shall I warm you, darling Beth?"

His mouth touched hers and her lips rose to meet the kiss. Eagerly, lightly, teasing, licking, tasting. Yes, he would warm her. She could never be cold again in his arms. Dimly, some thought about the cold was echoing in a far recess of her mind, but his nearness and his kisses were taking away all conscious thought. She was aware that he was sitting down on the wooden bench again and drawing her down to sit astride his lap. His hands caressed her urgently, like light-licking flame, seeking out her vulnerable, secret places, smoothing across her breasts and abdomen, stroking her inner thighs, the deliberate sensuality of his touch increasing as he reached the core of her womanhood.

"Griff," she found herself whispering. "Please . . ."

"Please what, my Bethany? Tell me. What shall I do to please you?"

His mouth was pleasing her. His hands. The strength and hardness of his body. The scent of him, taste of him. She wanted to sink against that hardness, draw it into her and make it part of her. But as this thought coalesced within the heat and wanting of her mind, another gust of wind tore against the walls of the sauna.

"The storm's worsening. Don't mind it, Beth. We're warm here." But his words pushed through her sensual languor and made her mind focus on the thought she had tried to form before. No, she and Griff were no longer cold, but the dogs—the dogs were still outside, hitched to the sleds in the worsening storm.

"Don't do that," he murmured against her ear. He could feel her slip away from him. Her distancing herself was pulling him back also, back to reason and reality, and he resented this. "Don't think," he told her, and at the same time told himself. "Just feel, Beth. Feel . . ."

But she had already pulled away from him, a little frightened at the passion that was still sweeping through her. "The dogs," she said, "I just left them . . ."

She had never done that—never! Even cold and wet and sick herself, she had always seen to her team first. What or who was Griff Deane to her that he should sweep away all that she had believed in with kisses and caresses?

"The dogs." She could tell that he, too, was taken aback. For a moment he said nothing as she gathered her clothes and dressed hurriedly. Then, he said, "I'm coming with you."

She shook her head. More than anything, she needed to put distance between herself and his disturbing presence. "There's no need. You need to get completely warm. I can handle the teams myself."

"I think I've told you before that I'm not in the habit of allowing someone else to shoulder my responsibilities." There was an edge in his voice. "Besides, I'm thoroughly warmed, thanks to you."

She looked at him quickly. His eyes, a dark sea-green in the dim light, held a trace of anger, impatience. She knew that it was for himself, and she knew why. Griff Deane had forgotten for a moment that the dogs were an important and expensive investment. Her own impatience swelled to match his. How could she have forgotten what he was like?

"Suit yourself," she said abruptly, then turned and left the sauna. She did not see the look in his eyes change to a kind of wry amusement, as if he laughed at a joke that had backfired against him.

Chapter Five

The storm was gathering ferocity when, dressed in warm, dry clothing, she made her way to where she had left the dogs. Unmindful of the storm, they had curled up in the snow and were awaiting her. Now, they greeted her with joyful barks and eagerly followed her into their kennel. She unharnessed them, talked to them, and praised them as the wind swirled around them. She was about to feed them when she realized that Griff had also come out of the cabin to help her.

They worked in silence, the shriek of the wind making conversation difficult. Bethany had to admit, as they secured the dogs in an indoor kennel against the storm, that she was glad to have Griff's help. Admittedly, she was tired and it was not easy to get through the feeding ritual in the teeth of the wind and the snow. Then, suddenly, she frowned. Surely Griff hadn't worn his sopping or frozen clothes into this storm?

She saw that this wasn't the case when they finally returned to the cabin. He was wearing an old parka of Piers' and a familiar-looking sweater and ski pants. He saw her looking and smiled in apology.

"I borrowed them when I found them hanging in a corner of your cabin. It was either borrow or put on those." He nodded to his sopping clothes, now drying by the wood stove. "I thought you'd forgive my wearing Piers' clothes under the circumstances."

She had forgotten she still had those things of Piers, and now she tried to recall how Piers had looked in the clothes. The bulky gray sweater had been Piers' biggest, but it barely stretched across the muscles of Griff's chest and shoulders, and the tight ski pants accentuated his length of muscle and bone. She could not recall how Piers had looked, but she remembered much too vividly the feel of Griff's strong body.

"That's all right," she said, speaking quickly against the treacherous memory. "You'll need dry clothing to get back to Tilikit."

To her relief, he seemed as anxious to leave as she was to have him go. "I'd better be going right away. I've been expecting a report from the company, and I thought that it'd be flown in today. I hope so, because I doubt that I'll hear anything more from New York until after this storm blows out." He walked to the window restlessly, stared out into the dark. "How long did you say Alaskan storms lasted?"

"About a week," she said, "and you're probably right. The storm will interfere with the radio transmissions, too."

He groaned. "What a god-awful place," he muttered.

Her chin went up, her eyes narrowed. "Nobody asked you to come to Alaska," she said.

"No, you're right." There was a hard glitter in his eyes as he added, "Well, we seem to have run out of things to say to each other. I've thanked you for coming to my rescue." He paused for a moment, long enough for confusion to sweep through her. Swirling through her present irritation with him was the memory of his kisses, the yielding of her body as he held her against him. But he seemed to remember none of these things, or, if he did, to hold them in no great account. "Since we've terminated our temporary partnership, I'll probably not see you for some time," he was going on. "You'll allow me to leave my team with you until I find other accommodations? Of course, I'll pay the going rates."

"Of course." It was business, pure and simple, as it was meant to be. As it had to be. "I'm sure that the Kobuks can help steer you to a more compatible partner."

Without another word, he gathered his wet clothes in a bundle and made for the door. As he pulled it open, a blast of wind and snow infiltrated the cabin, and high above the snow they could hear the wailing of wind. Talka is looking for her lover again tonight, Bethany thought, and shivered.

She almost called him back, but by then it was too late. He had gone through the door and shut it behind him, and in a moment she heard the muffled roar of his snowmobile above the shriek of storm. She watched from the window as his light transfixed the dark, and she told herself not to worry. "I've raced in worse weather than this," she muttered.

She wanted to turn from the window and get on with her life, but she couldn't. The rapidly receding flicker of light held her attention. Griff wasn't used to Arctic storms. He wasn't used to winds forty miles an hour packed with snow and icy rain. He didn't know the road to Tilikit so well. He *wanted* to go, she thought. I didn't make him leave. Nobody could make that man do anything he didn't want to do, and he can take care of himself.

But, as time passed, her anxiety grew. Bethany cooked some of the fish that Julie had brought her the day before, added a stack of sourdough pancakes then found she could not eat. The wailing of the wind seemed to have increased, become higher more intense. By now, surely, he had reached Tilikit. And if he hadn't? She visualized the seven-mile stretch between the village and her cabin at Lover's Run, and she bit her lip. Out of her worry and confusion, a thought surfaced: He came back to help me on the trail when he thought I needed help.

Abruptly, she got up from the table and began to pull on her heavy boots. This is insane, she told herself. He's not even my partner in a race! Yet, her fingers were clumsy with anxiety. She strapped the night-light to her forehead, pulled on her parka and two pairs of heavy gloves, and then let herself out of the cabin. Immediately, the force of the wind caught her and made her gasp. A tidal wave of icy snow hurled itself against her cheeks, and she narrowed her eyes to try and see her way. Visibility was zero. She couldn't see more than a few inches ahead of her in the gale.

I'm insane, she repeated, as she made her way to the kennel and called her dogs. Their hardy readiness cheered her, and she harnessed them rapidly to her sled. As she did so, her mind moved quickly. She'd make her way to Tilikit. If Griff hadn't arrived there, the Kobuks and the other villagers would help her search. If he were safe . . .

She paused. How am I going to explain my showing up there if he's already there safe and sound? For a moment, she thought of unhitching her dogs and going back into her cabin where she belonged. Then another howl of wind caught her, and she knew that she had to satisfy herself that he had made it back to the Kobuks.

"*Gee, Katiktok,*" she cried, and with the brave light of her headlamp bouncing against a vale of snow, they started out. They hadn't gone more than a hundred yards when she realized that the storm was even worse than she'd imagined. She knew the way to

Tilikit like the palm of her hand, and yet she was having trouble with disorientation. Someone like Griff could easily have been lost. "*Haw*," she commanded her dogs. "*Haw*, now, Freya, Katiktok, good dogs!"

She'd gone a good half hour through the snow when she spotted the light coming toward her. It weaved in and out of the eddies of wind and snow, burning bright, then blinking out, but her heart started pounding when she saw it. It had to be Griff. "Griff?" she yelled into the storm, but the wind took her voice and muffled it to nothing. All she could do was to head toward the glimmer. It, she realized, wasn't moving. It was quite stationary, quite fixed.

She was almost upon the snowmobile before she saw him. He was kneeling by the machine, heedless of the whirling snow. She knew him at once, even though she could hardly see his tall form. "Griff! Are you hurt?"

Some part of her shout got through to him, and he looked up and saw her. He got up at once and began to hurry toward her, the wind making him appear to stagger with its force. "Bethany!" he shouted, and then the wind tore away his words and she could only make out, ". . . snowmobile has a problem. No use trying to make it to Tilikit. Trying to coax it back to your cabin."

Julie had always said she preferred dogs to snowmobiles. "Leave it, come with me," she yelled, and saw him nod. He shut off the yellow eye of the snowmobile, and next moment he was on the sled beside her.

He bent to her ear. "Second time today you've bailed me out," he cried above the storm. "It's getting to be a habit, Beth. What made you come after me?"

She had no ready answer and was glad to have the excuse to shout to her team and urge them back toward Lover's Run and the cabin. The wind was at their back, now, and the going was somewhat easier. Guiding the team took most of Bethany's concentration, but she could not totally block out the effect of the tall, solid body wedged next to her in the sled. Why *had* she gone after him? It was a good question, but she had no answers.

Perhaps because of her preoccupation, returning to the cabin was no easy task. At one point, her sense of direction completely deserted her, and she was sure that they were going in circles in the blinding snow. Griff seemed to have no such fear. "This way," he said, and he spoke with such conviction that she obeyed his instructions without question.

Throughout the rest of that strange journey, they slipped into a tacit, intuitive cooperation. When they came to a long, steep slope made treacherous with ice, Griff took over the driving of the team, his strength effective an deterrent to any sudden surge on the part of the dogs that might cause the whole sled to tip. Later, Bethany walked ahead while Griff drove in the trail she broke through the storm. It was more than an hour later that they finally reached the cabin, and Griff reached out and clasped Bethany's gloved hand tightly.

She returned the pressure. They had made this journey together, and she shared his relief at the thought of warmth and safety. Without words, they cared for the dogs and then stumbled through the door to the welcome heat and light of the cabin. Safe, she thought, we're safe. We made it back.

"Bethany." She turned quickly and saw that he was watching her with an unreadable expression in his eyes. "I asked you before—what made you come after me?"

She had had time to answer the question in her own mind, but still she stumbled over the words. "I told you. Out here, people have to depend on each other. I saw how severe the storm was getting to be, and I was afraid that you didn't know the road to Tilikit well enough. I was afraid you'd gotten lost."

"I might have, though my sense of direction is usually pretty good, but before that could happen my gas line froze up on me and my snowmobile just died. I was trying to coax it back to your cabin, a bit at a time, when you found me." He came to rest his hands lightly on her shoulders. "Thank you," he said simply.

His touch was so disturbing that she had to fight an impulse to pull free of his hands. Before she could do so or speak, he was saying, "I'm afraid that settles it. There's no way I'm going to make it to Tilikit tonight. Tomorrow, if the weather eases, I'll drive my dogs to the village. Meanwhile, I'm afraid you have a guest."

She had been so concerned with getting them home, so wrapped up in her feelings and reactions to this man that his words caught her by surprise. Her eyes flew to his, her lips parted in denial. And then, common sense came to her rescue. Of course he was right.

It was no big deal. She'd spent cramped nights in strange houses along the dogsled racing trail, taken refuge from storms with other mushers during last year's Iditarod. Male or female, mushers were mushers; rivals but also companions. And she and Griff had been companions on the way back to Lover's Run just now. Companions and—she had almost said it—partners.

She turned away from him. "Of course," she said, trying to make her voice assume a matter-of-fact quality she didn't feel. "I'm afraid I can't offer you much in the way of a meal, though. Warmed-up fish and sourdough pancakes."

He grinned. "Try me. Being nearly frozen twice in

a day has whetted my appetite. I have a feeling I could eat a big helping of . . . What's that delicacy the Kobuks are fond of serving? Boiled whale skin?"

She laughed. "*Muktuk*, and it's really quite good."

"An acquired taste." His muscles rippled against Piers' too-small sweater. "Is that what you live on, Bethany? *Muktuk* and moose steak and canned food?"

She shook her head. "I freeze a lot of my own vegetables from the summer," she explained. "It's beautiful then. The whole area around Lover's Run turns green, and a lot of funny, spike-billed birds come to fish at the lake. I can have fresh fish and cow parsnips and greens—and then blueberry or currant pie sweetened with birch syrup."

"Beautiful," he murmured, but he was not thinking of the picture she painted. Her eyes were bright, her cheeks red from her battle against the snow and wind, and again he was forced to look at her as more than just a desirable woman. The thought disquieted him, made him frown down at the fish on his plate. She had made it plain that they could not be partners in the Rohn Relay, and that was all that mattered. All that *should* have mattered, anyway.

Everything about Bethany was a contradiction. Her body welcomed his want of her, but yet she resisted her own desire and his. She had refused his partnership, and yet she had risked herself and her dogs by coming out to look for him in the storm. Griff's frown deepened. When he had left the cabin hours ago, he had been relieved to get away from all the conflicting emotions this woman roused in him. And yet, back there by his stalled snowmobile, when he had seen her face framed by whirling snow, he had felt an exultation never before experienced.

"Did you have this cabin built during the summer?" he asked, wanting to clear his mind of these disturbing memories.

She smiled. "We didn't 'have it built' at all. Piers and I put the place together—all but the sauna, which I added myself later. The Kobuks helped us drag the one-hundred pound bags of cement, but Piers and I were the ones who rolled logs, and lugged the cabin ridgepole into place." She pointed to it with proud satisfaction as she added, "Julie helped me to do the 'woman's work.' We varnished the floors and walls. And I was put in sole charge of constructing our outhouse."

He shook his head. "All this to live in the wilderness. Did you always have this hankering after silence and isolation?"

"Isolation?" She began to clear away the plates as she went on, "I don't think so. I have my friends and the dogs and all of nature. I grew up in New Hampshire with a lot of creature comforts—perhaps too many of them. My father nearly killed himself trying to get rich while he climbed the corporate ladder. He was always hopping on a plane, going here or there, but in spite of all his money and prestige, I doubt if he or my mother was very happy. Maybe that was what pushed me into going the other way—made me want to live close to nature, away from 'civilized' ideas of wealth and profit."

"And your parents? I thought you said they lived in Florida. Did your father repent his evil corporate ways?"

There was a touch of cynicism in his voice and she frowned. "He had a coronary about seven years ago, and he was forced to slow down. Another attack completed his retirement." She paused. "He's not happy. He frets and fusses and wants to work again. I suppose the power and corporate glory is hard to give up."

"Old habits are hard to break." He picked up a dishcloth and joined her at her makeshift plastic-bucket sink, taking the dishes from her and drying them. His action was so easy and natural that she did not feel any surprise. "And you? Were dogs always a habit with you?"

She nodded. "I always loved them, yes. I loved anything that had to do with snow. Skiing, sledding, wilderness camping—I was into them all. When I was at school at U.N.H., I roomed with a girl who'd been to Alaska as a child, and she sold me on the north country. I think that's when I decided to come north one day and compete in the dogsled races. Then, my folks moved to Florida and I got a job at Mount McKinley National Park for the summer . . ."

"And met Piers." His hand touched hers briefly as he took a plate from her, and she suddenly saw the incongruity of the corporate head of Deane Enterprises drying dishes in her rustic cabin. Before she could comment, he was saying, "I can understand your love of the wilderness, Bethany. There would be a joy in relying only on yourself—which, as I once told you, is one of the qualities I learned early."

"From your father." He nodded, and she said curiously, "What did your mother think of that?"

He shook his head. "I don't know. My mother died years ago, when I was young. Perhaps if she'd lived, Dad wouldn't have been the loner he was. I don't mean he was without friends or women—there are types who'll always want to stick close to a winner—but my father never depended on them. He said that needing people was the path to hell."

His eyes were hard emerald, and he seemed to be reiterating a lesson to himself as well as explaining it to her. As always, she was conscious of his nearness, his power, the alien life-style and thought he represented. She was suddenly and acutely reminded of a

wolf she had once seen while driving her team home
at dusk: a great beast with eyes that flared green
against the dark, disdainfully regal in its aloneness.

"Do you believe that, too?" she asked, her voice
uncertain. He shrugged, and his intensity dissolved
in a smile.

"I'm aware that I need people's help," he told her.
"Which brings me back to this evening. We've both
had an exhausting day and we need to sleep. Do we
flip a coin to see who gets the bed, or do I play the
gentleman and huddle up in a blanket on the floor?"

She had never been so grateful as she was for the
matter-of-factness of his question. Carefully casual,
she shook her head. "No need to do either. I have a
very serviceable sleeping bag and several blankets. If
you prefer the bed, I won't mind a night on the floor."

He did not smile, but amusement welled into his
green eyes and the mobile corners of his mouth. "I've
never thrown a beautiful woman out of bed," he said.
"I wouldn't want to start now. The sleeping bag let it
be."

They were both very purposefully casual as they
prepared for sleep. Bethany found an extra pillow,
handed Griff blankets, went through a bedtime routine that culminated in blowing out the lamps and
undressing in the dark. The banked fires in the wood
stove warmed the cabin, and yet she felt cold as she
crept between the sheets of her bed. Each movement
on his part, each rustle or footstep, brought her
senses to full alert. Perhaps he was aware of her
unease, for he did not speak at all as he settled himself into his sleeping bag by the stove, and his "Good
night," was so short as to be almost brusque.

She responded in kind, lying tense in her cocoon
of sheets and blankets. It was eerie to lie alone and
yet not be alone. Her eyes had become accustomed to
the dark and she could see the long, dark shadow of

Griff by the stove. He seemed relaxed and comfortable, and for all she knew he was already asleep.

But she could not sleep. Perhaps it was Griff's presence, but more likely it was the aftermath of the emotion-packed day. So much had happened, she thought, so much had been said and experienced. She let her mind move slowly over the day's events, beginning with her refusal of him as a partner. He had been furious at her, and yet he had returned to help her, nearly frozen to death in the process. And she had tried to warm him—

Enough! her mind cried, as she thought of the sauna, and she twisted uneasily on the wide bed. What had happened had come about because of the tension they had both felt in the face of danger. If that hadn't been it, why would he have wanted to leave the cabin so abruptly?

Griff stirred in his sleeping bag. A great gust of wind hurled itself against the wall of the cabin, flinging gusts of snow against the window. Slowly, in spite of herself, she was falling asleep, and as she drifted into snow-deep sleep, she found herself confronting a truth her waking mind shied away from.

She and Griff had worked with each other today, truly worked together. In spite of everything that had happened between them, she had to admit that there was no man in Alaska who would make a better partner than Griff Deane.

Chapter Six

She woke into almost complete darkness. The only sound she heard was the howl of the wind. The storm had certainly not blown itself out, she thought sleepily; in fact it had increased in savagery. There would be no running of the dogs today.

The thought of dogs brought her awake, upright on her bed, suddenly remembering that she hadn't been alone in the cabin through the long night. But Griff's sleeping bag was neatly rolled and in a corner of the cabin. Griff himself had gone.

Had he left early without wakening her? Had he left in this storm? Bethany got out of bed and went to the window. Unable to see anything but the thick ice that had formed on the glass, she frowned for a moment, and then began to dress. Griff could no doubt fend for himself. She needed to get a move on, start the morning routine of bringing in water, feeding the dogs. What Griff Deane does is no concern of mine, she thought. He's probably back in Tilikit by now. This move was like him. He . . .

The cabin door banged open, and Griff appeared. He looked like a snowman, with snow and ice sticking to his parka and all exposed parts of his face. Ice had formed on his eyebrows and long lashes, and his breath had frozen above the muffler wrapped around his mouth. In his hands he carried two full buckets of lake water.

"Good morning," he said in answer to her surprised stare. "I saw that you were sound asleep and decided to pay for my lodgings with a few chores."

"How did you find the way to the lake?" she exclaimed. "You could have gotten lost in this gale." She felt a wave of guilt for having imagined he'd leave for Tilikit without a word.

He set down the buckets and began to peel off his outerwear. "There was no problem about the lake, but you're right that it's a gale. I'd originally meant to leave for the village first thing this morning, but now I'm not so sure it can be done. Some of those gusts must be pushing fifty miles per hour. It would be foolish to try."

She agreed, but that meant he would be here in the cabin all day, she thought. Then she pushed the thought aside. No way was she going to fear Griff's presence. He had made no move toward her, and he would not unless she allowed him to do so. She said abruptly, "I'm going out to feed the dogs."

"How about a division of labor? One of us can feed the animals, the other cook breakfast," he suggested.

"Good idea. I hope you're a dab hand with bacon and powdered eggs." She grinned suddenly at the surprise in his eyes but had to admit that he made a fast recovery.

"Done," he said, and then reached out to tuck a strand of her red-gold hair behind her ear. "Dress up warmly, Beth," he went on, his voice oddly husky. "I want you to be in good condition to digest my gourmet cooking."

The dogs came leaping to her, frisking delightedly to be out of their indoor kennels, leaping and diving through the snow. She talked to them, cuddled and praised and fed them, but she could not submerge her whole mind in them. Her mind kept slipping back to her last waking thought of last night. I can't tell Griff I want to be his partner, she thought, not after I refused him. Much better to let things go on the way they are now. But though the thought made sense, it didn't particularly make her happy.

Perhaps it was this that created the tension that grew between them slowly through the day. It was not an overt tension, but one that rippled more and more insistently in the back of their minds, in what they did not do or say. Outwardly, they were busy. Snowy days, Bethany told Griff, were spent in readying for the next big race, in this case the Rohn Relay.

She showed him one of her preparations, a "dog bootie" made of leather. "It's to protect the dogs' feet along the trail," she explained. She thought he might laugh, but he only nodded and asked to see how the booties were made. When she demonstrated, he was quick to make some booties of his own. When she said that more than a thousand would have to be made to protect tender feet on the trail, he raised a wry eyebrow.

"Just as long as nobody in Deane Enterprises ever learns that this is what I did during my trip out here. They think I'm insane enough, chasing a team of dogs across frozen wastelands. To picture me making booties contentedly by the fire would make them call for the padded wagon and a straitjacket."

She chuckled, but as he handed her his latest creation, she was aware of the touch of his fingers. The old pull that had been between them from the first was gaining strength and power in the enclosed world of the cabin. "Your secret is safe with me," she told him, and saw the glint of emerald in his eyes.

"You're a woman of discretion," he said softly. And then, as if it were dragged out of him, he added, "A remarkable woman, Beth. I wonder if you know how remarkable?"

A treacherous pulse was beating in her throat.

Don't, a part of her pleaded, and yet another voice within her, a soft, hidden, insidious voice begged him to go on. She said aloud, briskly, "Watch it, Mr. Deane. Cabin fever might be getting to you."

He rose restlessly, his tall, powerful body seeming to fill the room with a restless, impatient virility. "Do you ever get cabin fever, Bethany Sheridan?"

He was standing so close to her that all she needed to do was stand to be in the circle of his arms. Her inner tension threatened to ignite and burn away her resistance, and she must not let this happen.

"Naturally," she countered. Casually she rose while managing not to touch him. "When that happens, I go outside. It's too stormy for a run, but the dogs still like some attention."

He looked surprised. "The dogs?"

"Yes. They're not pets, but they aren't just animals or investments to me. They're friends." She paused. "Perhaps that sounds odd to you."

"I'm finding that a lot of odd things make sense in your wilderness world." He shook his head. "Last night when I realized Deane Enterprises wouldn't be able to contact me for at least a week, the thought didn't bother me as much as it should. I have a feeling it's your influence." He did not reach out or touch her in any way, but the look in his eyes was as palpable as a caress. I must get out of this cabin and away from him, she thought. Then, he deliberately broke the tension by smiling. "By all means let us go outside and frolic with the dogs."

They spent some time in the stinging cold and then returned to the cabin breathless and with ice-cold cheeks. Things seemed easier on the surface, and Bethany was careful to keep this casual mood between them. Griff insisted on taking his turn to feed the animals while she cooked chunks of fish in a thick stew for their own meal. They ate listening to the wild keening of the wind, and the sound wound into her mind and thoughts, making her edgy. She would have dearly loved to take a relaxing sauna, but she did not dare suggest it for fear of the memories this might arouse in both of them. That is, at least, memory in her. Since their outing with the dogs Griff had treated her with a kind of detached politeness. When she suggested an early bedtime, he acquiesced at once.

"Perhaps the storm will lessen during the night," he said, when they had doused the lights and had retreated to their sleeping places.

"I doubt it. If anything, it will get worse." She had never minded storms before, but she had never had to share her cabin with Griff Deane before. In the darkness, she could hear him chuckling as he spoke again.

"Don't let that bother you." Again, surprising her, was that note of husky tenderness. "You're safe and warm and out of the storm."

But was she? Warm she was, but she did not feel safe, and the storm seemed something that could not be contained out-of-doors, but a wild, living thing that churned within her, destructive of her inner peace. The wind's screaming blended with her thoughts, and she was conscious of a great loneliness. I know how Talka feels looking for Nonak in the storm, she thought drowsily.

When she slept, she carried the wind's keening with her, and she dreamed that she was out in the snow. She was lost, and she didn't know the way back to her cabin. Snow danced around her like taunting laughter, and in the dark beyond the snow she thought she could make out red, threatening wild eyes. "Help me, I'm lost!" Bethany heard herself cry, but the snow fell thicker and the red eyes came closer. Now, she could hear low, mocking laughter.

"How can you be lost?" she thought someone whispered in her mind. "You're the one who likes to be alone and free." And then, the red eyes closed in on her.

She woke trying to scream, the cries like gasps erupting from her mouth. Her body was rigid with fear and with running, and she felt as chilled as if she were still lost in the snow. Worse, the red eyes had caught her, were holding her. With a waking cry she tried to tear loose.

"Bethany—Beth!" She realized that it was Griff who was holding her. "Wake up! You're having a nightmare."

She shivered and went limp against him. "I dreamed I was lost in the snow."

Another gust of wind hurled itself against the cabin, and she buried her face against his shoulder. Still caught in the horror of the nightmare and the drowsiness of awakening, she did not register that the warm shoulder against her cheek was bare. All she cared about was that his arms were strong and that his shoulder and chest were hard and unyielding and safe.

"No wonder, after all the excitement of yesterday," he was saying. "Delayed reaction, Beth." She felt a hand smooth back her hair, a tender, soothing caress. "Are you all right, now?"

Her senses were dulled with sleep, but in that unguarded moment all her own defenses were down and she knew his thought, knew that he wanted nothing more than to leave her and return to his own spot by the fire. She could not bear so soon to be bereft of his arms, and burrowed closer against him. Now she drew in the unique scent of him—wood smoke and the aftershave fragrance that blended with his own clean male scent.

"It's awful, being lost," she whispered against the

hard, warm world of him, and felt his hand pause in her hair, press her head closer against him for a moment. There was something so intimate in that moment that she was surprised when he spoke in a calm, matter-of-fact voice.

"I know exactly how you feel. I was lost myself, once. Oh, I don't mean last night in the snow. It happened when I was a boy. I'd been playing hide and seek in the woods near my father's summer cottage, and I wandered off and lost my bearings. I spent hours trying to find my way back home. It was dark, and the moon came out and made ghosts of the trees."

"Oh, poor Griff!" In her sympathy for that little boy, she came fully awake. She realized, also, how closely he was holding her, and tried to draw away, but he held her to him as if unaware of her reflexive movement.

"I was terrified by the time my father found me. Do you know what he said? He told me I mustn't allow myself to be lost again."

"How cruel!" She struggled from his arms and faced him in the dark cabin, saw that his face was faintly lined with light against the greater dark.

"Not cruel, Beth—realistic. And honest. Since that day I have never allowed myself to be lost—or at a loss in any situation. That is, until I met you."

Carefully, he ran the knuckles of his hand down the line of her cheek, around her delicate jawline, and lightly traced the outline of her lips. And with the touch it all came back—the tension, the electricity, whatever it was that pulsed, had always pulsed, between them. She tried to speak, tried to inject reason and sanity back into the moment but could not. Within the boundaries of her flannel nightgown, her body felt as though all the movements of nerve and blood and thought had stilled. Were waiting. She shifted in his hold, and her palms briefly touched his bare chest, and the silent waiting seethed into a swollen, liquid desire.

"Do you know what I mean?" His voice was husky, almost raw with sudden urgency. She wanted to shake her head. Don't tell me, don't show me—please leave me be! Instead, she found herself nodding. "Of course you do," he whispered. "It's been like this for us since I first saw you outside your cabin. Maybe as far back as Laconia, we've wanted each other."

Yes, she wanted him. Wanted him shamelessly. Was it possible, this incredible, this wrenching desire? Her breasts were swollen with it, her nipples distended into taut, yearning buds. She desperately tried to marshal her thoughts, her reason, then almost cried out as he dropped his arms from around her and moved away. Instinctively, her body followed his, curved toward him.

He did not kiss her, did nothing. "Tell me," he said roughly. "You tell me, Bethany. Say that you want me, have wanted me also."

"You know I have." Her admission was a low murmur he had to stoop to hear. And hearing it, he felt his heart leap in exultation. An exultation that turned to excitement as she bent and brushed her open mouth against his bared chest. It was a quick, almost shy kiss, an uncharacteristically humble offering, and he felt the white heat of his desire for her change imperceptibly, glow into something new.

"Beth." His voice lingered on her name and she shivered at the sweetness of the sound. "Tell me what would please you. Tell me what you want." Slowly, gently, he began to stroke the slender curve of her back, and she murmured deep in her throat as his lips grazed the lobe of her ear and his tongue touched a sensitive spot. "I want to make love to you. Do you want that also?"

She whispered, "Yes," and with a quick, graceful movement pulled her nightgown over her head and dropped it to the floor. She realized that he was already unfettered with clothes as he slid his long legs and powerful body under the quilts next to her.

In spite of her desire for him, she tensed. In the familiar warm world of her bed, his maleness was something alien, a little threatening. To her surprise he did not pull her immediately against him, but continued to stroke her tenderly and without demand. As his sensitive fingers brushed the line of her neck and arm and caressed the slender bones of her shoulder and back, she felt herself relaxing against him, realized that she was adjusting to the presence of his strong-muscled body.

Now, he began to kiss her, his mouth as light as the flutter of a butterfly's wing. It was a controlled lightness, for she could sense the leashed passion behind the small kisses. Her own mouth opened under them, and their kisses deepened into an intensity of taste and touch that urged a greater closeness. His hands relearned the contours of her body, stroked the full slope of her high breasts, eased the demanding pout of her nipples with the palms of his hand.

She murmured her pleasure as his mouth moved to where his hands had been. He sipped, savored, drew in the honey of her breasts and then moved lower, smoothing the taut, slender line of her abdomen and stomach, caressing her thighs down and then upward to find the warm satin of her womanhood. There, he paused in his enjoyment and worship of her.

She felt the strength of that worship mingle with her own desire, felt it rise through her like a wave of warmth and need that swept her free of any thought except of him. "Griff, come to me, please," she whispered. "I want you to love me. I want you to love me now."

He came to her, kneeling above her for a moment before she wrapped her arms around his neck and drew him down to her. Once more he kissed her, the delicate features, the parted lips. His tongue tested the perimeter of her mouth, then began the sweet invasion that preceded another.

He gasped her name as she drew him deep within her, and he felt the melding of his hardness with the rippling warm satin of her. He felt that he was drowning in her, and he wanted to drown as fire in groin and body screamed for release.

Yet he hesitated, waiting for her own response, looking down into her upturned face. In spite of the dark, he could see the luminosity of her eyes, the warm, sweet curve of her lovely mouth. She called his name and moved against him, and he held her tightly. Tightly, as if he could not bear to let go of her again.

She felt his arms hold her closer, cried out with the pleasure of his swift, initial strokes within her. But that was not all that made her hold him to her.

Somehow, as their bodies took their pleasure, she felt another melding, a completion of a joining that had begun long before this moment. Griff was right. Since their first meeting, this moment had been inevitable, inescapable.

No matter what came of this, she gloried in Griff's love. It was a little like coming home.

Chapter Seven

She woke to a feeling of warmth and well-being and instinctively turned in the wide bed seeking him. He had been such a part of her warm, sleep-sweet world that at first she didn't realize that he was not there.

He had not been with her for some time. His side of the bed was cool, and someone had stoked the wood stove. Had he gone outside again for water? But when she sat up in bed, she saw him standing by the window, his face turned to the storm.

He had heard her movement and he turned to her now, and something in his face stopped her from calling out a good morning, made her catch the bed-clothes against herself more closely. "Did you sleep well?" he asked. "No more nightmares?"

"No." She felt her nakedness acutely. Last night, the act of going to him had seemed natural and good. Now, seeing the expression on his face, her nerves and emotions felt exposed and raw. Her body remembered his lovemaking. Her mind realized that he regretted it.

He turned back to the window. "The storm seems on the wane. I'm going to ride into Tilikit after I've helped you with the dogs. I should at least try to do something about that snowmobile."

"All right." Suddenly, she wished him gone. She wished that he had never come, never intruded into her life. She wanted to dress and be about her everyday life, wanted a return to normal as soon as possible, but she hesitated to dress in front of him. As if divining her difficulty, he reached for the parka by the door.

"I was about to get water," he said abruptly, and began to pull on his outerwear. She realized that he was wearing his own clothes today.

The clothes had dried, the incident of the overflow and the storm was over. She dressed quickly when he had gone and began to prepare the dogs' morning meal. Their whole time together had been a mere incident in Griff's life, and that was how she, too, must see it. The physical pull between them had been too strong to be long denied, but now it was over and she was free of it. Perhaps Julie's right, she thought. I've been alone too long. Something was due to happen and it did—that's all.

She was feeding the dogs when he returned with the water, and without speaking they fell into the rhythm of the morning. Griff knew what to do as well if not better than she did, Bethany thought wryly as he helped her in the kennel and then returned with her to the cabin to prepare their morning meal. There should have been an air of sharing as they sat down to their mutually cooked meal, but the atmosphere was oppressive between them.

Neither of them broke the silence until a wind hurled loose snow against the window. The sound startled Bethany, and she said, "Are you sure you can find your way to Tilikit in this weather?"

"Quite sure." His tone was pleasant but brooked no argument. "After all, we're sure to experience worse weather during the Rohn Relay."

She nodded. "Yes," she murmured, "we will."

Instantly, his head came up, the intense green eyes looked into hers. "Do you realize that this is the first time you've said 'we' in connection with the relay? Have you reconsidered your decision, Bethany?''

She frowned. Instinct made her want to deny this, but she hesitated. Into her indecision he said, "I want to assure you that I have great respect for your skill as a racer. I think we work well together on the trail, and I also think we complement each other very well. We've trained together for a week, and it's a shame to waste all that valuable time." He paused. "I bring this up because I know you've been thinking the same thing."

Could he have read her mind? He was right. She could not dissemble with this man, and she nodded. "I have been thinking about it, yes. We do work well, and we reacted well together under stressful conditions." Her eyes rose to meet his as she added, "But there are problems, as you obviously must know."

He shrugged dismissively. "You're talking about last night, I take it. I agree with you that it mustn't happen again."

She was reminded of the look he had had on his face this morning, and something small and unreliable within her twisted in an odd, dull pain. He was continuing, "We're very much attracted to each other. As you pointed out, that's natural, working as closely as we've been working. But I'm in total agreement that business and pleasure can't mix. They never do, successfully. If you agree to the partnership, that's all we'll be—partners."

He spoke so surely that she felt a flash of irritation. So Mr. Griff Deane felt he had been in total control of the situation, had he? She said, coolly, "That much is for sure. I'm not the kind of woman who enjoys casual affairs, and I'm not looking for any other type of relationship. I like the life I've built for myself too much. As long as that's understood, I'll be your partner for the Rohn Relay."

He wondered why he did not feel more pleased at her acquiesence. Perhaps it was the hard look in her eyes, the same eyes that had been warm and luminous with feeling as she lay in his arms. He felt a ripple of regret, instantly supressed. He must not allow himself further involvement with Bethany Sheridan. "Good," he said aloud. "Then we agree."

He held out a hand and she took it, wondering at the odd light that flickered in his eyes for a moment, turning them to the color of evergreens in shadow. Then, he smiled and the look went away. "We've sealed our partnership," he said agreeably, and she frowned. Griff acted as if he had just won a battle for his corporation; no doubt that was how he saw their merger.

They harnessed their teams and she drove with him as far as his still-stranded snowmobile. Then, watching him drive his dogs on to Tilikit, she swerved her team and took them on a long run through the lessening storm. It was invigorating to be out in the cheek-numbing cold, good to expend her strength and energy in this way. She stayed out a long time, returning to the cabin only when she and the dogs were wearying.

She hummed as she fed and cared for her dogs, took in wood for the stove, hacked off a steak of moose meat for her dinner. Then, once inside the cabin, she began to straighten up, luxuriating in the feeling of being alone and pleasing only herself. The feeling lasted until she found, on a chair, the neatly folded ski pants and sweater that Griff had borrowed from her.

Instantly, his memory leaped into focus, no shadowy silhouette against the rough cabin wall but tridimensioned, fully fleshed, bold, for the garments that had been Piers' now carried Griff's scent and his imprint. For a moment she held the clothes, and then she carried them to a corner of the cabin and put them deep into the box she used to store extra clothing. "There, partner," she muttered. They had set the terms of their agreement, and as far as she was concerned she was going to make sure that these were carried out to the letter.

This decision was mutually adhered to during the next weeks. They were punctilious about spending each working moment in practicing racing techniques, in trying new approaches that would shave precious time off their runs. Then, after their runs were over, they would spend time in discussing the rough spots of the day.

These discussions were often carried out over the Kobuk family table with everyone joining in. At other times, Griff and Bethany had long private talks in the cabin at Lover's Run. At first wary, Bethany soon realized that Griff was no longer thinking of her as anything but his racing partner. And, as time passed, she realized that she was beginning to enjoy his company. He was as skilled as she, and dedicated to the sport, with an intuitive quality that surprised and delighted her. Moreover, he had a strong sense of humor, and could take in stride such contretemps as dogs who chewed through the gang tether, or bad weather that caused delay and loss of time.

"I knew you'd be glad you took him on as a partner," Julie Kobuk once exulted. "Now, do you see what I mean? I told you he was a winner." Bethany agreed, and yet a small corner of her mind was not yet totally relaxed about Griff. It irritated her that even while he seemed completely easy with her, there was a small kernel of doubt and tension still locked within her. She tried to reason it away, but it wouldn't budge. Yes, their association was one of business and Griff was the best partner she'd ever

had. No, he had not made one overt gesture toward
her, spoken no word. Yet, that tension remained and
flared at every given excuse, such as when he
touched her accidentally in their daily routine, or on
the occasions when she turned suddenly and caught
him watching her with that odd, unreadable expression in his sea-green eyes.

She refused to give in to this foolish unease.
Instead, they took longer runs together, worked
harder. The Kobuks were positive that Griff and
Bethany would bring the Rohn trophy to Tilikit, and
began to refer to it as "our trophy."

"It could very well be theirs, too," Griff commented as they rested one afternoon after a long and
grueling morning's run. "I have a feeling that the
Kobuks have adopted me—Eskimo style. Elmer and
Julie fuss over me as though I were Tony or Giuliana."

"Eskimos are like that," she agreed. "They're
raised with a lot of love themselves, and so they raise
their children with love. It makes them special people."

"Yes," he said, and paused. "I suppose love does
make for special people." Something in his deep
tone made her look at him, but the expression on his
face was merely thoughtful. "Well, if we're to win the
trophy for the Kobuks, we'd better get back to work,
partner." He stretched his tall, powerful body as if
suddenly restless, and she felt a quickening of that
never quite absent tension in herself. "Bethany," he
then said, "isn't it time we started practicing for the
relay? I've got an idea that might help us hone our
timing skills."

"Go on," she said, and he outlined his plan. They
would separate with both of them driving in opposite
directions for about ten miles.

"That would put you near the road between Tilikit

and Raedar, and I'll be right at Shiny Mirror Pond. When I get to the pond, I'll turn and race toward you and the road—meet you there."

"And once we meet I'll head for Shiny Mirror Pond, and we can check our times." Bethany liked the idea. Like most of Griff's thoughts it was simple but effective.

The "relay" began very well, with Bethany driving her team and waiting at the road. It was a clear, fine day and the team, anticipating some new excitement, was impatient to be off. So impatient that when Griff was seen coming toward them, Bethany could hardly control her dogs. Her shouted commands had no effect on them, and in battling to get them under restraint she lost several precious minutes of time. She wasn't satisfied with her run, and when Griff pulled up beside her at Shiny Mirror Pond, she told him so.

"You'd think that I could control my team after all this time," she said, frowning her dissatisfaction, and was surprised to see his grin. "What's so amusing?"

"I'm just glad you didn't see my progress to the road." Humor glinted in his eyes as he called softly to his dogs and left his sled to come to her. "Your dogs almost got away from you—they left me by the side of the road! I wanted to save time, so when we got to a steep hill I got out and pushed the sled from behind. I guess I succeeded only too well." He paused. "Guess what happened?"

She began to laugh. "They took off on you?"

"There I was yelling and hollaring on top of the hill, and there *they* were, going like sixty! It looked like a scene from a comic strip." She whooped with laughter, and he seized a handful of snow and threw it at her. "It's not kind to laugh at a fellow musher."

Without pausing in her laughter, she mounded a

snowball and let fly at him, catching him accurately on the shoulder. The dogs looked on, mildly amused as their humans began a seemingly demented game of firing snow at each other. Bethany gave as good as she took, but in the end there was no contest. Griff maneuvered her against a tall spruce, his eyes sparkling like gems in the Arctic half-dusk as he held up a large handful of snow.

"Surrender or die," he said with a laugh.

"I surrender—I think." A movement of her shoulders jarred loose more snow from the tree behind her, and she shouted in indignation and jumped forward, landing against him. For a moment they stared at each other, and she saw that quick shadowing of his eyes, the beginnings of a frown on his face. For a second longer he held her, and then he dropped his hands.

Their laughter had stilled suddenly, and she did not know where it had gone. Carefully casual, she began to walk back to their sleds. "You don't need to impress me with your timing," she told him. "If we keep going the way we've been going, we'll win at Rohn."

He nodded, but so slowly that she glanced at him. The frown had intensified, but he was not looking at her at all. Instead, he seemed to be staring into the middle distance as if he were looking into his own thoughts. "Yes, of course, Rohn," he said, after a moment. "We'll certainly win the Rohn."

They started back toward Lover's Run in an odd silence that was in complete variance with their earlier, easy mood. She was grateful for the silence, grateful for the chance to pull her thoughts and defenses together. The chance touch had unsettled her more than she cared to admit—had startled and upset him, too, if she wasn't mistaken. The spark of tension within her blazed higher as she remembered the expression in his eyes and face. She wondered if he would make any mention of it when they reached the cabin, but he did not.

Instead, he told her that he would be late for their morning run. "It's the day I meet the plane from Anchorage," he explained. "The negotiations with Halstead are getting to a particularly tricky stage, and I'm anxious to make sure that some decisions I've made have been implemented."

"Of course. I'll start without you, and plan to be at Shiny Mirror Pond around noon. If you can make it by then, meet me there." She was proud of her casual tone.

They went together to feed and tend to the dogs, and for the first evening in many weeks they worked in almost total silence. She wondered what Griff was thinking. Probably his mind was already on the corporate wheeling and dealing that made up another facet of his life. Now she could hear him whispering to his dogs and something inside her that was raw and unhappy rubbed against the boundaries of her heart. No matter what, Griff was not "just" her partner. He was a corporate mogul and she had better not forget it. He was just temporarily her partner. He was . . .

She frowned suddenly. Though the other dogs were milling close to her, Katiktok was not among the pack. Her favorite was usually the first to beg her caresses. "Katiktok?" she called.

There was no answering whimper, no warm, wet muzzle against her sleeve or hand. Frowning, Bethany shone her flashlight about the kennel. In one corner, huddled miserably, lay Katiktok.

"Katiktok?" Fear shrilled Bethany's voice as she hurried across the snow and knelt down beside her lead dog. In the flare of the flashlight, Katiktok's eyes were glazed and missing their usual alert look. Seeing Bethany so close she whimpered, but couldn't get to her feet.

"Beth, what is it?" Griff's voice behind her was sharp with concern. "Is the dog hurt?"

As if in answer to his question, Katiktok lifted a foreleg and licked feebly at her paw. Was she hurt? But what could cause such glazing of the eyes? Suddenly, Bethany knew. She bent down, her nose almost touching Katiktok's paw.

"Antifreeze," she whispered. "Oh, my God, antifreeze. She's poisoned, Griff—we've got to get her to a vet, or she'll die."

Chapter Eight

Griff carried Katiktok from the kennel and into the cabin. Bethany followed, her words pouring from her. "While we waited at the road, she must have stepped in some antifreeze that had leaked out of some old truck and remained on the ground. She's licked it off her paws, Griff. The stuff's poison to dogs . . ."

"Is there a vet we can get her to?" Griff demanded.

"In Raedar, but that will take so long and Katiktok could be dead by then." She stared down at her dog who was twitching, her eyes vague and lost. "Antifreeze gets inside a dog's kidneys and causes crystalline substances to form inside. That blocks the kidneys and will kill Katiktok."

"Isn't there something you can do for her now before we drive her to Raedar?" His hands came down on her shoulders, gripped hard. His voice was hard, too, cool, devoid of her almost hysterical fear. It forced her to think, to pull together her control.

Alaskan dogs had no titer—no immunity against disease, for few bacilli existed in this climate. Katiktok would die of this sweet, deadly substance unless she could think of something.

"Bethany?" Griff's voice was still cool with an almost deadly control. "You've bred dogs. You know about them. Take your time and think," he said quietly.

She frowned, remembering. Once she had heard of another musher's dog ingesting antifreeze. "Ethyl alcohol," she cried. "He poured ethyl alcohol down the dog's throat and it flushed out the antifreeze."

"Do you have any around?" He let go of her and yet it seemed as if he touched her still, steadied her. She went to the medicine cabinet on the rough wall, opened it, and groaned to see the bottle was only half-full. "This isn't enough. It wouldn't be nearly enough."

Even so, she was on her knees beside Katiktok. Griff held the dog's mouth open while she poured the strong liquid down Katiktok's throat. All too soon, the precious fluid was gone. "Perhaps there'll be some in Tilikit," Griff said. "We'll head that way. We'll make good time on my snowmobile."

Bethany began to nod, and then another memory seized her. "Ethyl alcohol or vodka. Vodka works as well in a pinch. I've got some in the cabinet. Piers used to like to drink occasionally . . ."

They got the vodka down Katiktok's throat while they were carrying her out onto the snowmobile. The dog weighed close to fifty inert pounds, but Bethany supported Katiktok in her arms as Griff started his snowmobile roaring into the darkness. They had never traveled so fast, and Bethany gasped as the air seemed to shatter in frozen chips of ice and hurl itself against her face. "Hold on, Katiktok," she whispered, as the dog whimpered in her arms. "Hold on, sweet dog. Griff will get us there."

The surprising part was that she completely believed this. There was a tense determination about Griff that would not admit the possibility of defeat or failure. And, when they roared into Tilikit some moments later, he pulled immediately up to the Kobuks' door.

"Tell me where the vet lives in Raedar, and I'll

bring him. You pour vodka down Katiktok." A brief smile touched his lips. "If I know the villagers, there'll be plenty of bottles of vodka around. Tell everybody I'll buy them cases of the stuff later."

He did not wait for her consent but bent and touched her icy cheek with his fingers. For a moment, his green eyes met hers, a brief, shimmering glance that brought his name involuntarily to her lips. He seemed to hesitate then, uncertain for the first time this night. But before he could move or speak, Julie had opened the door of her house.

"What's happening out here?" she demanded in horror. "Griff, what's the matter with Katiktok?"

"Bethany will tell you." He was already moving to his snowmobile, long legs eating up the distance. "I'll be back soon, Beth, I promise."

She held the promise tightly to her as the Kobuks roused other villagers and scouted up bottles of vodka. If she hadn't been so concerned about her dog, Bethany would have appreciated the humor of the situation, especially as some villagers were somewhat reluctant to part with their cherished booze.

"Old man Nogeak practically cried when I told him the stuff was for a dog," Elmer explained, as he poured a half-bottle down Katiktok. "Said he'd been saving the bottle for a special occasion, and he was sure this wasn't it." He paused. "How much of this stuff you going to give this poor animal, Bethany?"

"As much as she can take. There's no way to get rid of the antifreeze except to flush her out completely." Her heart ached for Katiktok's glassy-eyed suffering, and she whispered, "Don't give up on me, sweet dog. We've been through too many good and bad times for you to die. I won't let you!"

"She doesn't look too good to me, Bethy," Julie said worriedly. "When will Griff get back with that vet?"

"He'll come as soon as he can." Mentally, she pictured Griff roaring into Raedar, ousting the vet from a deep sleep. But supposing the vet was elsewhere, had been called to aid some other suffering animal? "He'll find him, he'll come," Bethany avowed stoutly.

As if in answer to her words, there was the sound of Griff's snowmobile roaring outside. She leaped to her feet and ran to the door to open it, then found herself caught in Griff's arms. Behind him was the bundled form of Raedar's vet, Dr. Ivarson. As the vet moved quickly to examine Katiktok, Bethany whispered, "I knew you'd bring him."

"I had a hard time finding him." In spite of the cold that had reddened Griff's cheeks, his voice was warm, almost tender. "He was setting a dog's broken leg for one of the Raedar people, and I had to run him down. Once he heard what you'd been doing for Katiktok, he wasn't worried. Said that was all he could do, anyway." He paused. "How is she?"

Katiktok was glassy-eyed as Dr. Ivarson examined her. "I'm not sure," Bethany whispered. "Griff, I can't stand to lose her. I raised her; I love her. I should have checked her feet when we got back from our run. I should have known!"

"Hush." She realized that he was still holding her, for his arms tightened. "How could you know? Don't try to second guess what happened, Beth." He let go of her to put a finger under her chin and raise it. "It's going to be all right. Trust me."

"The assurance of Griff Deane, corporation head?" She tried to smile, and he smiled also but shook his head.

"I'm speaking as your partner." Gently he added, "Some things are beyond our control. All we can do is hope."

She turned to stare at him, but before she could

fully register the expression in those green eyes, Dr. Ivarson called her over.

"You've done a good job here, Bethany," he said. "It's going to take some time to know for sure, but I think you've licked the foul stuff in Katiktok." He added that he and Griff would transport the dog to his office in Raedar so that she could be observed through the night. "I want to put her on intravenous feeding as soon as possible, and I want to monitor her progress more closely than I can do here."

Because Bethany could not bear to leave Katiktok, Elmer Kobuk started his cranky snowmobile and the two of them followed Griff and Dr. Ivarson to Raedar. There, Bethany was relieved to observe that although Katiktok was still very sick, her eyes had regained some life. Even so, she and Griff stayed at the vet's for several hours. Elmer Kobuk would have stayed too, but Bethany insisted he return, and Griff reiterated his promise to buy cases of vodka for all those who had "transfused" Katiktok.

"I'll tell old man Nogeak. He'll be able to have a few hundred parties this way," Elmer said, grinning, as he took his leave. "You take care of Bethany, Griff."

Bethany felt Griff's hand rest on her shoulder, lightly and yet with complete assurance. "It will be my pleasure," he said quietly.

It was very close to four in the morning when Dr. Ivarson finally pronounced Katiktok out of danger. "She's going to be disoriented for a couple of days, but she'll make it," he said. He insisted that Griff take Bethany home. "Otherwise, you'll need to get a people-doctor for this one, here."

Bethany had been going on sheer nerve for some time, and the relief that followed Katiktok's safety was her undoing. She felt fine enough when they left Raedar, but along the road between Tilikit and

Lover's Run, she found herself so sleepy she couldn't keep her eyes open. Sleepiness in a dogsled rider was an enemy; for one sure way of getting killed was to fall asleep at the reins and tumble from the sled, thus suffering injury or suffocating in a snowdrift. She fought against her drowsiness until Griff stopped the snowmobile and took her in front of him.

"Go to sleep, Beth," he told her, and the very quietness of his voice seemed a lullaby that rocked her to sleep. She did not fight drowsiness any longer but leaned against him, her head pillowed against his shoulder as he slowed the snowmobile and guided them both to the cabin.

She knew they had reached the cabin when she heard the dogs barking. I have to wake up she told herself—and could not. Her legs and arms felt like leaden things that could not function. Her tongue felt thick as she tried to explain. "I don't know what's happened to me."

"It's called being human." He stopped the snowmobile and got out, lifted her easily into his arms. "You've been under a terrible strain, Beth. You'll be all right after a good, long sleep."

She leaned her cheek against his shoulder. It felt so good to stay like this, and a warmth filled her as he opened the cabin door. This was how it should be. The cabin had been so empty without him.

He stopped to light a lamp, and the glow of it wakened her somewhat. She realized that he was carrying her across the cabin to her bed. "I'm all right," she protested, but he paid no attention, only set her on the bed and knelt down to undo her boots. She said, "Griff, there's no need. Really. I'm perfectly capable of taking off my own boots. And you must be as tired as I am . . ."

"You talk too much, Bethany." One boot came loose, and she felt the warmth of his hand curl around her foot. "Relax. All this comes under the heading of caring about a partner. Weren't you the one who said that in the wilderness people had to take care of each other?"

"Yes, but . . ."

But his presence called to her, reached deep within her and stirred unbearably the rapidly growing vortex of tension. No, not of tension— desire. She could not escape the knowledge of that want as he knelt at her feet. Couldn't he feel it? she wondered. Her heart was pounding so hard against her rib cage that she was sure that he must hear it. But he simply pulled off her other boot and then looked up into her eyes.

In the lamp glow there was a luminosity about his eyes. "Will you be all right, now?" he asked, and his voice was low, the husky voice she had heard earlier in his arms. She nodded. "I'd better be going, then."

I don't want you to go. She had not spoken them, but the words lay heavy in the air between them. All this long while of working together, of seeing, some- times touching, all these long days of denial rose in her heart, in her mind. Griff, I want you to stay here with me.

"I don't want to go." He said it quietly with a casu- alness that rode on the edge of a tension at least as great as hers. His eyes had changed, grown dark, and the base of his proud nostrils flared as he strove for control. "I will go if you want me to, but I don't want to leave you, Beth."

How to answer? Her lips moved, sounding out rational words. You know what you decided between you, her reasoning mind accused. You know. But she was powerless. She could not make herself say the words, could only look at him.

And he, looking, saw the struggle on her face and the parted, vulnerable mouth. The lips were tender for him, and so were her eyes. Wide and velvet-soft in the golden spill of lamplight, answering his question with silence. He felt shaken, compelled against the urging of his reason and his better judgment, and beside the fire that raged through his senses he felt a wonder that was all tenderness. Carefully, gently, he drew her to him and held her gently against him.

"Forget what I said, my Beth. You're exhausted and so am I. Sleep a long time and don't worry about Katiktok. I'll be going now."

She heard him say the words and they made no sense. The words he did not say spoke directly to her heart. *I want to stay with you, Beth. I'm going now because I want you so.* All weariness fled from her as she wound her arms around his neck, drawing him to her.

"I'll sleep better if you stay," she whispered.

"Are you sure?" But he knew she was sure. He was kissing her with swift, passionate kisses and she was responding to them, her lips seeking his mouth as he kissed her temples and the curve of her mouth and the rounding of her chin. Then, drawn at last to the source of warmth and desire, their lips met, touched, tasted. Her teeth nibbled his lower lip, and she murmured his name deep within her throat as their tongues warred sweetly, seeking out the familiar treasure of each other's mouths. Now, his hand moved down over her body, strong and sure and seeking the rounded thrust of her eager breast.

Clothes—there were too many of them. It was almost a fire in her blood to push aside the layers of warm clothing and find the sweet, supple strength of his muscled body. They accomplished their undressing between long, mind-drugging kisses, until, impatient but triumphant, she reached the last of her garments.

"Let me," he told her. The depth of his voice was

as tactile as a caress, and so were his hands resting for a moment over her barely clad breasts before he removed the flimsy barrier. His mouth moved with concentration, seeking the soft valley between her breasts, rubbing his cheek against the generous inner curve before his lips and tongue curled sensuously around her nipples. She sighed deeply, trembling with a satisfaction felt deep within her as he savored her, suckling and teasing, circling the taut peaks of her breasts.

She pressed his dark head against her, holding it there, never wanting the warm drawing sweetness of his mouth to cease. But already she wanted more. Greedy for the ecstasy she knew they would taste together, her body moved closer to his, undulated sensuously against his hardness. One of her slender hands crept across the furred bareness of his chest, down over his flat, taut belly and onto his thigh. Then, back to caress his lean flanks, his muscular buttocks, around again to caress the still-clothed hardness of him.

The groan deep in his throat was almost a growl of pleasure. He covered her hand with his, pressing it against him. "I have wanted you," he whispered.

He had wanted her too. How could she have doubted it? She moved closer to him, wanting his kisses, wanting him, but he held her a little away. "I know what we agreed, and I have kept my word, Beth. But not now, not tonight." He bent to her lips, his mouth claiming hers, his tongue a welcome marauder. "Differences don't matter tonight," he muttered against her lips.

She tugged at his remaining garments and he aided her while sliding from her the last scrap of clothing she wore. In the glow of the one lamp she drew in the strength and power of him, the breadth of shoulder and muscled hardness and the passionate vigor that was his.

She leaned back onto the pillows and drew him down with her and when he spoke again his voice was husky. "I want this to last a long time for us, love, and yet I find I can't wait. My Beth. It's been too long, being without you."

"You needn't wait." At her whisper he smiled at her, a sweet, tender smile in the midst of their passion that reached deep within her so that all that she was and all that she had glowed open to him, turning to him as a flower responding to the sun. She encircled him with her arms as her body welcomed his.

They were matched so perfectly that their bodies seemed not two but one. He was a part of her and she drew him within her, welcomed and caressed the strength of him. And he, tasting her sweetness, was lost in the honeyed warmth of her. He whispered to her: fragments of love words, murmurs that even he could not understand. And as they joined in lamp glow and shadow, she answered him in kind. The fire that burned them both rose, blazed, coalesced, and shattered them within its heart, melding them in a crucible of passion. And it was then that she found the words formed in her heart: Griff, I love you. I love you so.

Chapter Nine

She came awake from a dream of elemental warmth and comfort. It was as if she had been sailing on a warm and sunlit sea. She had never felt so safe, so sure of happiness, and as she lay feeling wonder seep through her, she knew the source of her joy.

He lay close to her, his great body curled against her, one arm wrapped around her waist, the other under her head and cradling her head. She felt his breath against the nape of her neck and wondered if in all the world there was a moment as sweet as this—a moment of awakening in Griff's arms. And then another thought came swiftly, cutting across her pleasure and her happiness, a memory. Once before, she had lain in his arms and awakened to see his face cold, shuttered, remote.

As the thought and memory touched her mind, she felt his lips touch the nape of her neck, then move sensuously to find a secret, sensitive spot behind her ear. "My Beth," he murmured.

His voice was still hazy with sleep, but the sweetness in it took away all her fear. She pressed herself against him, moving back and hips into his accommodating hardness.

"Good morning," she murmured. "It's late. Did we really sleep so long?"

"Too long, to my way of thinking." His hand was stroking her breasts suggestively, the palm teasing already erect nipples. "Why sleep when there's so much to learn about each other? I want to learn more about you. I've already gained incredible insight . . ."

"Like for instance?" She turned on her back and smiled into his eyes. They were lazy, half-hooded, content. He ran the tip of his thumb lightly around the perimeter of her mouth.

"For instance, I like the taste of your lips." He bent to sample her mouth and whispered, "And you do something incredible with them when we kiss."

She chuckled both at his nonsense and for happiness. It surprised her, filled her with wonder that was a little like sunlight. She had been content before, happy here in her cabin, but she had never felt so joyous, so alive. All her senses were alive and eager for new knowledge of him and their world together.

"You talk a lot of foolishness," she said, but softly, unable to stop smiling at him.

"Don't shoot me down when I'm enumerating your charms, Ms. Sheridan." Lightly, his fingers traced the curve of her breasts. "I find your body exquisite, giving, quite extraordinary. Your breasts are tipped with warm coral, or sweet wild strawberries . . ."

His voice faded as he bent to kiss her breasts, and she sighed deeply with pleasure and with the rise of desire that moved within her. His want of her was obvious, but he did not seem in a hurry to continue their lovemaking. Instead, he prolonged the sweet torment at her breasts. She ran her hands down his smooth shoulders, felt the tension of muscles beneath the warm skin, and smiled. Two could play at a game.

"Since we are partners," she said quite seriously, "I think I deserve equal time. I've found out things about you, too, Griff. This . . . and this." Her lips moved lightly from his mouth to his smooth shoulders, touched the flat male nipples, charted the hardness of his belly and the concavity of navel. But when her mouth strayed lower, nibbled lightly against his rock-hard thighs, he stopped her progress by lifting her atop him so that she straddled his strong maleness.

"It seems that we've discovered a great many things," he whispered. "Shall we learn more—together?"

"Agreed. Oh, yes, Griff." She gasped at the initial thrust of his passion, the warm hardness against her softness which was like a completion of herself.

They took their time, loving slowly and with delicate tenderness, their bodies fitting so well, moving so easily together as if each nerve end, each cell and drop of body's blood intuited the wish of the other. They touched, kissed, refreshed their loving with age-old love words that seemed yet new to their lips. You are so beautiful—I have wanted you so, needed you—I need you now.

Later, they dozed again, arms holding each other close, and woke to warmth and closeness that had gentled now that the sea of passion had ebbed away. She lay in his arms, his forehead against the top of her head, her cheek against his shoulder. She felt him sigh deeply, and heard the beat of his heart.

"Why?" she murmured, for the sigh, and his arms held her momentarily closer.

"So much for all my good intentions. As I think I began to tell you last night, I'd wanted our partnership to keep within the guidlines we set. It wasn't easy, being with you, working with you, but I struggled mightily to keep my word."

"Why?" she said again. Now that it had come about, this inescapable loving, she thought of all the time that had gone before as wasted time. "I wanted you too, Griff; though I couldn't bear to bring myself to admit it. I suppose I was a little frightened."

"My turn to ask you why." He rolled a little away from her, half sitting up in bed and looking down at her. The lamp still glowed down on his powerful torso, and sunlight splashed through the window and covered the bed with brief, Arctic light.

She struggled to find the right words. "Oh—we're from such different worlds. You represented values and thoughts I can't believe in or share." A trace of frown had appeared between his brows and she added, "It's true, isn't it? Could you share my life here?"

Instead of answering, he pushed back the bed-clothes and got up. For a moment sunlight glinted on his proud nakedness, the sleek male power that made the small cabin seem even smaller. Then, he reached for a towel and wound it around his loins.

"I have nothing against your wilderness paradise, Beth. Where else could a man start his own sauna?" Playfully, he tousled her hair. "Since I'm a gentleman, I'll even start baking those stones for us if you promise to meet me in there."

By the time she met him inside the sauna, clouds of white steam were rising from the hot stones. She sluiced cold water over him, eliciting enraged howls and the revenge of being thoroughly kissed while he washed her down in turn. Their bathing was long and sensual and should have culminated in love-making, but did not. As Griff said, the dogs needed to be fed, and then they were needed in Raedar.

"As I mentioned to you, my plane comes in from Anchorage today," he reminded her. "And Katiktok is probably waiting for you anxiously."

He was right, and yet she sensed that it was neither business nor dog that caused Griff's sudden restlessness. She felt it herself, had felt it the moment she spoke of the difference between them. And yet she could no longer deny the longing she felt for him, nor could he deny that he cared for her. Perhaps he read her thought because before leaving the cabin to tend the dogs, he pulled her into his arms, his green eyes intense.

"It will work out, Beth." His mouth was close to hers but not touching. "Trust me."

"How can I not trust my partner?" she smiled back at him, and he kissed her lightly, then with greater passion. "If we keep this up, the dogs will never get fed and your plane will never be met," she whispered.

"I'm tempted to say to hell with the plane." But he did not. In half an hour the dogs were fed, and Bethany was harnessing her team to her sled.

They had decided that Griff would drive his snowmobile into Raedar while Bethany drove her dogs. "I want you to be with me, but there's no telling how long I'll be delayed by business," he said regretfully. "I'm going to need to draft several letters and instructions to my people, and more than likely it'll take some time. I know you want to visit Katiktok and then take the dogs for a long run." He paused, then added, "I'll get to Lover's Run as soon as I can—by evening, for sure."

She felt a satisfied warmth at his words, felt it spread through her as she called to her dogs and headed them toward Raedar. But when he had passed her and his snowmobile had dwindled away into the distance, doubts that had not pressed upon her in his presence now began to trouble her. It was easy for him to say that differences didn't matter, that they added zest to their relationship. But what did Griff want in that relationship?

For that matter, Bethany asked herself as she skirted Tilikit and turned onto the road that led to Raedar, what do I want? It wasn't an easy question to answer, and it was still with her when she arrived at Dr. Ivarson's small clinic.

There the doctor put her mind at ease about Katiktok. The dog, he said, was recovering very nicely and could go home in a few days.

Bethany's eyes filled with tears as she hugged Katiktok. The dog whimpered her joy as she licked Bethany's face with an abandon that was in marked contrast to her apathy of last night. Realizing that Katiktok should rest, however, she thanked the vet for his care of Katiktok and prepared to leave. Dr. Ivarson shrugged away such thanks.

"Nonsense. I'd have done the same for any dog I found on the road let alone a valuable racing dog like this one. I told your friend Griff Deane the same thing when he explained the animal's value last night." He paused, chuckling. "Of course, I don't need to tell you that his being head of that big Deane corporation surprised me. You don't see big business tycoons running dogsled teams too often."

Bethany nodded. She wondered why she felt a stir of uneasiness. So Griff had mentioned Katiktok's worth to Dr. Ivarson. Why not? she argued with herself. Katiktok *was* a valuable animal.

"Anyway," Dr. Ivarson was continuing, "he was really concerned about the dog not being able to run the Rohn Relay. He said he'd sunk a lot of time and money into assembling the best team of dogs and getting the best partner for the event, and he didn't want to lose it all now because of some antifreeze."

Bethany smiled, but the vet's words were like a cold and hard stone against her heart. She tried to argue against that hard coldness as she drove her dogs through Raedar. Why should she be so upset? she argued with herself. Certainly, people had the right to different values and different priorities. Yet, instinctively, she knew that Griff's words to Dr.

Ivarson had gone far deeper and to the root of the differences that separated them. Griff hadn't, as she had once thought, acted quickly to save the life of a dog she loved. He had moved swiftly to preserve an investment he'd made in the Rohn Relay.

He wants to win, he needs to be the best, she thought. The wind stung against her eyes and made them smart. That's the way he is, and he'll never change. Power and gain are what're at the heart of him and he doesn't need anyone—certainly not me.

She had meant to take her team on an easy run today after yesterday's excitements, but her own churning thoughts and emotions caused her to strike out across the vast frozen lands to the northwest of Raedar, an area where she seldom ran her dogs. The terrain was harder, the icy slopes steeper and more treacherous, and she was grateful. Because she needed to keep her wits around her and concentrate, she didn't need to think too carefully about her feelings for Griff. And yet she remembered that through the sweet madness of last night not one word of love had been spoken by Griff. If she'd read anything else into their lovemaking, she was to blame.

And now what? Bethany's throat tightened into a raw, harsh sob she couldn't control. If we stay together as partners, last night will happen again—and again, she thought. I can't let it. I'm already halfway in love with him—and he's not for me. We'd be terrible for each other, a disaster. I must stop it before it's too late to turn back.

"Tonight we'll talk," she said aloud. The words seemed to echo bitterly against the desolation of the landscape through which she drove her dogs and the misery of her mind. "Tonight I'll tell him that—that we can't be partners. He won't like it, but it'll have to be."

As she spoke she realized where they were. She

had started the run much later than usual, and it was pressing toward evening. Against the Arctic darkness, the unfamiliar territory around her looked strangely ominous. "Time to go home," she said out loud to the dogs. "Gee, now, Freya—home!"

The sky was clear and the air dry, but a wind began to whip itself up into a frenzy and spread a thin sheet of old snow through the icy air. Through this she drove, eyes narrowed and intent on finding her way. She was halfway home when the sled suddenly jolted, then jolted again. There was a sharp crackle of ice, a yelp from the lead dogs, a sickly squealing.

Reining in as hard as she could, she shouted for the dogs to stop. The frightened animals would not obey until they had pulled her forward several more yards into icy water. As they did so Bethany heard a choking gasp from one of the dogs and saw that not all her team was on its feet.

In her concern Bethany moved without thinking. She got off the sled, too late realizing that they had hit a giant overflow. As she sank knee-deep in icy water, she tried to find her footing, fell backwards. By the time she had managed to find her feet again, she was soaking wet. Worse, one of the dogs lay inert in his traces. It was young Aladin, and as she called to him and examined him she realized that he was dead.

Her heart caught in her mouth. As they had hit the overflow, Aladin must have slipped in his traces. Momentum had dragged the poor beast forward, and he had suffocated with snow and ice water and slush. Bethany moaned as she loosened poor Aladin's traces, and the other dogs pressed close, sniffing, whining at the smell of death. Freya threw back her wolflike head and howled, the mournful death knell echoing through the icy dark. "Poor Aladin," Bethany whispered. "Poor fellow."

Now she realized that her teeth were chattering. She needed to get to warmth before she, too, froze to death. Already her hands were turning numb. She had an idea that she was not too far from Lover's Run, but she also knew that she needed to use all her skills and experience and get back to the cabin as soon as possible. If she fell by the roadside, her team would be lost like poor Aladin, here on the sled beside her.

"Let's go!" She called to her team, and her voice cracked with urgency. She had to make it—and she would.

It took less than half an hour to return to Lover's Run, and by that time she could hardly feel parts of her body. Her toes were long since numb. She turned her dogs loose in the kennel, then stumbled into the cabin, stripping off her wet clothes and pulling on woolen underwear, sweaters, blankets, gulping hot coffee from the kettle on the wood stove.

The coffee did not warm her. Neither did the brandy that she laced it with. Her hands were tingling and weak and she was suddenly and sickly exhausted as well as bone-deep cold. It seemed as if the freezing wind and ice had eaten a hole right to her marrow and no warmth could touch her ever again. When the stove and liquids didn't warm her, she crawled under the covers of her bed, curling into a fetal position to conserve warmth. Even this did not warm her.

The thought of her unfed dogs filled her with guilt, but when she tried to move to go to them, her teeth chattered and her legs would not carry her. She prayed that Griff would come, as he had promised.

But he did not. Finally, she forced herself to pull on her boots and hobble outside with dry food which she dumped into the dogs' feeding dishes. When she returned to the cabin she was so dizzy she could not stand, so cold she felt as if she were breaking apart. I'll have some more brandy and swallow some aspirins and go to bed, she told herself. Maybe sleep would come and warm her.

But when sleep came it was more unconsciousness than sleep, a heavy, sickly coma that did not give her rest. She struggled out of it hours later, alternately shivering and blazing with heat. I have a fever, she thought dumbly, but could not move a muscle to reach for water even though her throat was parched.

Her helplesness both frightened and angered her. She couldn't be helpless—not out here. I've had fevers before, she thought. I'm going to be all right. She forced herself, with an effort of great will, to sit upright in bed, and found that the walls and floor of the cabin tilted, grew great and small, like mirrors in a carnival fun house. She got out of bed and fell promptly to her knees, helpless with vertigo.

Outside she could hear a muffled roar. Griff? she wondered, fuzzily. Was that Griff's snowmobile? Had he come?

She saw the door of the cabin open as if in slow motion, and Griff was standing there. "Good Lord," he exclaimed. "What is it? What's wrong with you?"

Through stiff lips she tried to tell him. She realized she wasn't making much sense, that she was jumbling things, but she had to make him understand about Aladin, and the overflow, and the long ride home. He came to kneel beside her and lifted her into his arms, and his face was paler, more frightened than she had ever seen it.

"You're burning," he muttered. "God, Beth—why? Taking the dogs so far when you were alone."

The word "alone" jarred some buried thought and she murmured disjointedly, "Alone—always alone. Too different, Griff. We're too different."

The darkness seemed to act like a vortex, sucking

her down into it. Frightened, she clutched at him,
whispered his name. She saw his eyes for a moment,
heard him calling her, and then she was lost in the
greedy, circling dark.

Chapter Ten

When she opened her eyes again, she was lying on her bed. Dimly, she registered that Griff had divested her of boots and clothes and that she was in her nightgown. She was also unbearably thirsty. But before she could say anything, he was there beside her, his arm around her shoulders, a cup of water in his other hand.

She drank thirstily, then sank back against his shoulder. She could focus on his face, now, and the green eyes were narrow slits of worry. She tried a smile. "I'm all right. I've had colds before."

"It's no cold and you know it. You damn near froze to death." The arm around her tightened. "I should get a doctor down to look at you, Bethany, but I don't like leaving you again."

She closed her eyes, too tired and too sick to deal with anything except the fact that he was there with her. "I'm used to being alone," she whispered.

"So you've said." There was a grim note in his voice as he lowered her to her pillow. Almost perfunctorily he pulled the covers up around her neck, tucked her in. "Bethany, do you have anything besides aspirin in the cabin? You've got quite a fever."

"Never get sick . . ." but she drifted away on the last words, her eyes closing as the greedy, spinning

dark sucked her back under. She was dimly aware of
his shaking her, talking to her urgently.

"I'm going for the doctor. Listen, there's water near
you and I'll be back as soon as I can." Then his face
and voice, too, drifted away and were lost.

He was back in the cabin when she surfaced once
more, and so was a man she recognized as Dr. Tully
from Raedar. But something was wrong with both
Griff and Dr. Tully. They became very tall, then
shrank to nothing. She felt dizzy watching them, and
so she closed her eyes. As she did so she heard Griff
say something about pneumonia but could not catch
the doctor's reply.

Pneumonia? she wondered tiredly. For a long
while she seemed to hover between terrible heat and
bone-chilling cold. She was in the storm looking for
Griff, but she could not find him. She called his
name, called—and perhaps he'd been there all along
because she heard him say, "Hush, my love. I'm here.
I'm right here."

He was holding her, and she pressed her face
against his chest whispering ragged words of explanation. Why she had been out in the storm that day,
why Aladin had died, why she felt that they could
never really be partners. "Too different, too different," she moaned, but all the time she kept her face
against his unyielding chest. She felt so sick, but
somehow it was better when Griff held her.

Heat and cold—and Griff forcing her to drink liquids and medicine. She drifted along for how long
she did not know, but there was a time when she
started awake, gasping and struggling and searching
for breath. She couldn't find it, couldn't find it, and
she could only make deep, wheezing notes deep in
her throat. She could not even call for Griff, but he
was there. He lifted her out of bed and carried her

across the cabin into the sauna and sat with her in the hot moist air.

Slowly the strangling hold on her windpipe lessened, and she could breathe again. She was aware, dimly, of his talking to her as he held her, assuring her that he was there and that she would be safe.

"You'll be all right, my Beth, because I'm here," he told her. "I'll keep you safe."

She was surprised at his voice. There was no confidence there, none of his usual decisiveness. Instead there was a terrible fear and with it grim determination. "You'll be all right. I need you, Beth. *Need* you . . . I won't let anything happen to you."

She felt herself relax against him, let his arms rock her gently against his hard chest. She drew a clearer breath, another, gratefully pulling the moist air into her lungs. And as her exhausted body tumbled back into sleep, she held to herself a conviction that nothing could touch her while Griff held her so.

Someone was singing in the room. Slowly, carefully, Bethany opened her eyes. There was no confused blurring of light and darkness but only the faint light that streamed in through the cabin window. Even this gentle light hurt, and she blinked. As she did so, a figure near her bed moved.

"Bethy, you awake?" Julie Kobuk said.

Bethany was aware of an instant and almost overwhelming disappointment. Griff, her mind cried out. She had expected to find him there, just as she had always found him when she slipped in and out of consciousness. Could she have imagined him?

"How long have I been sick?" Her voice came out a raspy croak.

"Nearly five days." Julie had been sewing something, and she put it down and clumped over to Bethany's stove. She filled a bowl with something and brought it back to her bed. "Some soup, like you're going to need to build back your strength," she said. "I promised Griff I'd make you eat when you woke up."

"Griff." She hadn't meant to repeat the name aloud, but her lips formed the name. Julie nodded.

"He's been right here, Bethy. All the time. I offered to help with the nursing, but he wouldn't hear of it. The doctor told him what to do." She slipped a pillow behind Bethany's head. "We were afraid you had pneumonia, but you were in such a bad way we didn't dare move you to the hospital in Anchorage. For a while there, you were one sick woman."

Lying there listening to Julie's voice, Bethany wondered at it. Griff had cared for her and nursed her for five days. Her heart moved on a swift, involuntary flutter of gladness.

Coaxingly, Julie spooned a little soup and held it to Bethany's lips. She tasted it obediently, and found that it was good. The big woman nodded approvingly. "He's a good one, Bethy," she then said. "If I were you, I'd nab him quick. Men like him don't often happen by Lover's Run. You two could win every race together—and I don't mean just dog-sledding, either."

Bethany frowned. Something was nudging at her newfound content. She did not want to think of it now, but remnants of thoughts nagged at her. Were Griff and she suited? He had held her close and sworn that he would keep her safe. And yet, there was the other side of the coin, the differences that no amount of care and kindness could remove. "I wonder," she murmured.

Julie said, with heat, "You're two of a kind. Proud and stubborn. Loners. You belong together!"

Bethany said nothing more but sipped the soup. Perhaps Julie was right, she thought. Perhaps this brush with illness had clarified things for them both. "I need you," she had heard Griff say to her. God knows she had needed him, still did! Her heart seemed to hush and catch its breath, then leap with gladness as she heard a familiar sound outside the cabin. Julie put down the soup bowl with a grin.

"Now look what the cat dragged back again! I sent him to get some sleep, and here he is again." Mischief filled her dark eyes. "Wonder why he came back, eh?"

Before Bethany could reply, Griff was striding through the cabin door. He seemed to bring the outdoors with him: the crisp, clean scent of wind and snow and pine, the vigor of the open spaces. His eyes went to her face, searched it, and for a moment she saw the blaze of pure joy in it. But when he spoke his voice was merely pleasant, almost casual.

"So how do you feel?" Griff asked.

"As if a sled ran over me." She wasn't sure whether she was disappointed by his tone or not. He smiled at her, but there was something about the smile that didn't tally with the memory of strong arms, the frightened yet determined voice grimly set on protecting her against disease and death itself. "How do you feel?" she continued tentatively, and Julie gave one of her loud, disapproving snorts.

"How *would* he feel after nearly a week with hardly any sleep?" She put her fists on her broad hips. "I suppose you came running out here to make sure I was doing my job."

He shifted his attention to Julie. "Naturally." The smile he gave Julie was the same easy one he had offered Bethany. "I wanted to make sure that my partner was on the mend. I do need to protect my investment, Mrs. Kobuk."

Julie just laughed as if at a joke, but Bethany felt a sickening tightness within her as if some blossom

alive and open and glad had suddenly felt a spear of
frost. She looked searchingly into his lean, dark face
and saw that he meant what he said.

Investment—she and Katiktok and the Rohn Relay
meant time and money to him. "Of course you
couldn't afford to lose a good partner now," she
heard herself say, her croaking voice even harsher.
"I'm sorry I'm more trouble than I'm worth."

"I wouldn't say that." He did not move closer to
her but away from her, seeking a chair farthest from
her bed. His eyes on her face were inscrutable. "Good
partners are hard to get."

Under the covers she clenched her hands into tight
fists. Her instincts about him had always been right.
She would eternally be grateful that she had not
believed Julie's romantic notions and made a fool of
herself.

"I owe you one, Griff," she said. She was proud of
her voice, now—the tone grateful but impersonal.
She tried to meet his gaze calmly and found that light
glinted on his dark hair, turning it to sparkling jet,
and limned his face with light. The line of his cheek,
the curve of his mouth stirred too many memories,
and she hastily turned away. "Both for me and for
Katiktok."

He grinned. "Katiktok's already repaid me. She
licked me all over when I drove out to the vet to bring
her home a little while ago. That's why I left you in
Julie's hands. I thought you'd enjoy seeing her when
you felt better."

"That was kind," she murmured. She meant it sin-
cerely, and yet his kindness bothered her. He was so
elusive, this man! No sooner did she feel she understood him than he changed again. By his care of her,
he'd even changed the decision she had made about
their partnership. It would be rankest ingratitude to
sever their business connection now.

She saw that he was watching her and that his eyes were dark, wearing that odd, shadowed look. Then, he smiled and the shadow went away. "Repay me by getting well," he said. "I want you back on your feet as soon as possible, Bethany. We've got a race to win."

Bethany did not see much of Griff during the next few days. Julie, who drove out each day to see her and help with the chores, explained that Griff's corporation was demanding most of his attention.

"From what I gather they'd like to have him in New York," she explained. "After all, he is the big boss." She added, "If you want my opinion, he isn't going because he wants to make sure you're well."

Bethany made no answer. Julie had brought the week's mail, picked up at the post office in Raedar, and she pretended to be absorbed in her correspondence. She wished that Julie would drop the subject of Griff's devotion to her. But Julie plainly had no such intention.

"He's worried about you, Bethy. Why else would he ask me to come by each day and be sure you don't tire yourself out? He wants you to get your strength back. He cares."

"He cares because he wants me to help him win the Rohn Relay," Bethany said.

"You're wrong there!" The big woman shook her head. "If he wanted that, he'd be hounding you to get back into training. The man loves you, Bethy."

Purest pain lanced through her, and for a moment she closed her eyes against it. Behind the shut lids exploded memory: Griff holding her after her nightmare; awakening in his arms; the safety of those arms when she was ill, his whispered words of love and defiance. All dreams—all misinterpretations. She pushed away the remembrances and with them the memory of his kisses, his caresses, the sweet weight of his body. Love? she thought. Not love, not on his part. Griff doesn't love anyone. He doesn't need anyone like that.

"You're wrong," she said quietly. Julie began to speak but then stopped, clamping her lips tight.

"Whatever you say," she sighed. There was a pause. "Do you want me around any more today, Bethy? I promised Giuliana I'd stop by her school on the way home from Lover's Run. She's in the school play and they're rehearsing," she added proudly.

Bethany hugged her friend. Julie Kobuk was so full of warmth and loving herself that she could not conceive of anything else in people. But, she thought as Julie left, she was wrong about Griff.

Griff— She paced the cabin restlessly. It was suddenly too small, too confining, and she resented that feeling. This had been her safe, her beloved world before Griff had muscled his way into her life. Now, even when he stayed away from Lover's Run, she felt his presence. Julie spoke about him. Tony, who came by every day to exercise the dogs and bring water from the lake, spoke of him admiringly, or brought messages from him. "Griff says you're supposed to take it easy for a few more days, Bethany. No runs or anything—you leave that to me." Who was Griff Deane to try and order her around?

Because she remained his partner, did that mean she had to kowtow to him as did his minions in New York? She felt warm with rebellion, with an anger that was making her feel stronger than she had since her illness. "You don't own me," she whispered angrily. "You do not own me, and you never will!"

She went to her window and looked out. The swift Arctic dusk had already closed in, but the weather was clear and stars were sprinkled against the shift and weave of the northern lights. It had been so long since she took the dogs for a run. "I'll bet Katiktok and Freya miss me," she murmured, and thought achingly of poor Aladin. She hadn't even trained a replacement for him. She felt well and strong. Why not go now?

Exhilaration rose in her with her decision, and she dressed quickly, pulling on boots and outer wear and fastening her headlamp around her head. She went to call her dogs and they came to her happily, licking her hands and frolicking around her. She harnessed them, taking more time than usual, for her legs were not as strong as usual and she felt a little humming in her ears when she bent down. But as soon as they were off and running, she knew she'd done the right thing. Wind and cold exhilarated her, made her blood sing.

"This is what I need," she thought exultantly. "This is what I've wanted all along!"

She would have dearly loved a long run, but after about ten miles sense told her to turn the team back. It was a wise move. In spite of her joy at being outdoors again, her strength had almost given out when she returned to the cabin. She felt a little giddy, as she came up the last mile and steadied herself by calling to the dogs.

"Gee, now, gee . . . good dogs, Katiktok, Freya!"

Suddenly, she saw a bobbing light coming toward her. Another racer on this same track? Surely, not. But then, in the clear cold air she heard his deep voice shouting. "Beth! Bethany, is that you?"

What was Griff doing here? She felt a swell of conflicting emotions: gladness that he was there and resentment that he was checking up on her. "What are you doing here?" she shouted.

He didn't answer at once but pulled his team around and waited for her. She couldn't see anything of his face, but when he did speak his voice was angrier than she'd ever heard it. "I could ask you that. Are you trying to kill yourself or just be sick again?"

"I'm not dead and I'm not sick. I'm a racer," she snapped back. "It was time I stopped coddling myself—time you left me alone."

"Oh, is that it!" The angry scorn in his voice made her wince. "What would have happened if you'd gotten sick on the trail and passed out?"

She passed his team in a whir of speed and drove on against a giddiness that had been intensified by her own anger. "I'll do as I please!" She yelled back at him, and the wind brought back his steadfast answer.

"Like hell you will. Not while I'm your partner, you stubborn woman!"

Not while he had money and time invested in her. Bitterly, she wheeled her team up to the kennel and stopped. Adrenaline was pounding through her, and it kept her upright as she dismounted. But he had sensed her tiredness anyway, and he was beside her instantly.

"Go into the cabin. I'll take care of the dogs," he told her. His voice had lost the overtones of anger, but the command in it had intensified. "You will be sick again, Beth, I mean it. You don't want that."

She knew he was right. She went back to her cabin and the warmth made her feel even dizzier. When that passed, she managed to pull off her boots and outer gear. Then, she slumped into a chair. He's right, she thought. It was an irresponsible thing for me to do. I should have made sure that someone came along with me that first time. Why am I suddenly acting like this? I know better.

The cabin door banged open. Griff closed it with his boot and stared at her for a moment. She looked, he thought, pale and worn in spite of the brisk cold outside. He had been so terrified when he found her gone that anger had spilled out when he found her safe—anger that muscled aside all the things he should have said. He did not understand why he was constantly at a loss for what to say, what to do with this woman. Softly, he swore and saw her head come up as her eyes met his.

"That *was* a truly stupid thing to do," she was saying. "I'm sorry."

He frowned. "What in hell am I going to do with you, Bethany Sheridan?" It seemed as if he were talking to himself. She looked a question and he added, "I'm due to leave for New York in a few days. I can't put it off any longer—my people need me to oversee a crucial stage with our negotiations with Halstead." He paused and added, "Now I'm worried that you may pull something foolish like this again."

"Don't worry, I won't." She felt weak and unhappy, and in order to conceal her thoughts she got up and walked to the stack of mail that Julie had brought. She had not opened all of it, and now she pulled a large, official-looking letter from among the correspondence. "Odd that you should mention New York," she said, with an attempt at a smile. "Here's one from the Big Apple to me. From the Sportswomen's Association."

"What do they want?" He had come to stand behind her, and she was aware of his tall, muscled body, the closeness of it. She slit the letter open and moved a little aside to distance herself from him, but he was still close enough to read over her shoulder. "They seem to be asking you to come and give a talk on dogsled racing," he commented.

"They do that often. It's one of those letters Julie and Tony call my 'fan mail.' I'll send them a polite refusal as usual."

"Why do that?" She turned to look at him and saw

a thoughtful, preoccupied look in his eyes. "From what I read they offer you a healthy honorarium and ask you to come at your convenience. Can you afford to throw away money like that?"

There was a faint hint of mockery in his voice, and she knew he was baiting her. "Of course I'd like the money, but it's not so easy to fly to New York just like that . . ." She paused, realizing what he was getting at. "No," she said abruptly. "Forget it, Griff Deane. It's foolish."

"Why? You're not yet strong enough to take your team on runs. Why not take a vacation and satisfy your 'fans' as well?" Green eyes gleamed like emeralds and the deep voice hummed to a low, persuasive chord. "You can fly with me. Since the Sportswomen's Association will pay your transportation, all you need to do is book a hotel room in New York for the duration. How long would you need to be in the city?"

"A few days. It says here they want me to give two talks. But—it's impossible, Griff. The dogs need looking after."

"Tony would be delighted to help you out, and the dogs are used to him." His eyebrows rose scornfully. "Afraid of the city?"

He meant, are you afraid of me? "Don't be foolish," she snapped, then realized what he was up to. "Don't try to manipulate me," she warned. "I don't even know whether the Sportswomen's Association wants me to come now."

"You can come with me into Raedar tonight," he offered. "I'll have our man in Anchorage telephone New York for you and get a confirmation." He was sure of his victory. "Come on, relax, Beth! You'll be all the better for a change of scene. Maybe you'll even meet some of the city types I do business with."

"I'll think about it." But she knew from the glint in

his eyes that he was sure she would go. She frowned as she thought it through. The offer to speak was sudden, but perhaps for this one time Griff was right. The money would come in handy to help with the upkeep of the dogs and with her own supplies. Even more important, she could do with a change of scene.

And perhaps a short time away from her beloved wilderness would right the sudden precarious imbalance in her world.

Chapter Eleven

❧

"Courage, Beth. Not all New York is like the airport."

Griff's voice was bracing, but she could not shake the feeling that she was totally out of place. The Air Alaska flight from Anchorage to Seattle had been comfortable, and so had the connecting United flight to JFK. But the airport was jammed with so many people that she felt hemmed in, almost claustrophobic. Her senses were constantly assailed by glaring lights, shrill voices, loudspeakers. The mingled scents of the airport were unfamiliar, and underfoot she felt not the crispness of snow or the spring of a wooden floor but cold concrete.

Though it was barely December, a huge and garish Christmas tree winked on and off. It was no fragrant spruce but a tree fashioned of nylon and wire, and the sight of it made her suddenly homesick.

Griff was maneuvering her through the crowd, one hand on her shoulder. "You'll feel better once we get to the limo. Ah, there's Hal."

A dapper, middle-aged man was coming toward them, hand outstretched. Griff introduced him. "Beth, meet Hal Bluett, my right-hand man at Deane Enterprises."

Hal Bluett's smile was pleasant. "That's quite a compliment, but I wouldn't take him too seriously. Griff is the kind of man who insists on knowing what his right and left hands are doing at all times."

Outside the airport a uniformed chauffeur was waiting beside a sleek gray Cadillac. Bethany, who until now had thought Griff meant to take the airport limousine, noted the deference with which the chauffeur greeted Griff, who leaned back into the comfortable car seat and stretched his long legs.

"I'm not going to bore Bethany by talking too much business," he said as the noises of the airport fell away, "But have you done as I asked, Hal?"

The middle-aged man nodded. "I've booked your usual suite at the Sheraton Centre. Ms. Sheridan—Bethany, if I may?—has a suite on the floor below yours. It overlooks the city so you'll have a good view." He paused. "Griff, I'm sorry to say that your first meeting with the Halstead people takes place an hour from now. I knew you'd want some time to yourself, but it couldn't be helped."

"Of course." He glanced at Bethany in apology. "I'm sorry. I'd intended to show you some of the sights or at least take you to dinner on your first night in the big city."

There was genuine disappointment in his voice, and she was astonished by it. No doubt, she thought, he felt sorry for her because here she was gawking at everything like a genuine *cheechako*. She shook her head quickly.

"Please don't worry about me. I'm going to be busy, too. As soon as I get to the hotel I have to contact a Faye Contras, my contact person from the Sportswomen's Association." She paused. "However, I'm not sure about your booking a suite for me. I'm not sure about New York prices, but . . ."

"No need for you to worry. I get a special rate for my conferences," he replied smoothly. "The Sheraton Centre will be as convenient for your business as mine. In fact, you can walk out of the door and almost step onto Broadway. Not that you should do anything like that at night. There are more dangers here than in Alaska."

"I'll keep that in mind." He meant well, no doubt, but it was irritating to hear him telling her what to do in that high-handed way of his. He sounded as if he were making some unshakable rule about corporate business, she thought, as he turned to Hal Bluett and asked questions about the current position with Halstead. As Bluett briefed him, Bethany noted that Griff sounded more and more like a business mogul who was coming home to his familiar turf.

She shut out their conversation by turning her head and looking out of the limo window. As they glided into Manhattan she was entranced. The city was huge; bigger and much different from anything she had ever seen before. Though she tried hard not to act like a greenhorn, she had a hard time keeping herself from staring at the streams of pedestrians, the spate of traffic controlled by flashing lights on every street corner.

Griff turned his attention back to her as the limousine slowed. "We're nearly there," he said. The change she had earlier noted in his voice had intensified, leaving it crisp and totally businesslike. "Here's where you take New York by storm."

That would take some doing. To her mind the lobby of the hotel appeared monstrous. There was an amusing little café in the lobby, with a rendition of the Eiffel Tower, and there were also many people who seemed to be walking or standing about. A gray-suited bellman came to attention as the desk clerk recognized and greeted Griff with respectful cordiality.

"I'll make sure your suite is all right before I go on to the meeting," he told her, then stood aside for her as the elevator sighed open before them. The civilized courtesy made her smile, and she remembered how they had often brought in water from the lake together, chopped frozen moose steaks or logs, fed dogs, and sewed dog booties by the fire. He'd never have bothered with "ladies first" at Lover's Run, but this hotel and this city were not her world; they were his. Perhaps he read her thought for he smiled. "Don't worry about it, Beth, just enjoy the difference," he said.

Her suite looked out and across the bright, lively city. The view satisfied Griff, but though she could not put her finger on what bothered her about it, there was something. It came to her later, after Griff had gone, that her uneasiness sprang from the fact that the suite was just too big. It was larger than her entire cabin, and it was much more luxuriously appointed. Yet, at the same time, it conveyed to her a sense of aloneness.

"I've been in the wilds too long," she said aloud as she hung up her clothes: her trim but severe suit for the talk, a dress, slacks, and a sweater. The slacks were out of style, the sweater looked too heavy in this elegant chamber.

She telephoned her contact person from the Sportswomen's Association immediately. Faye Contras was delighted to hear that she was in New York and that the trip had been a good one.

"I know you want to rest now, so I won't bother you tonight," she said, "but I'll pick you up at the Sheraton Centre early. About nine, or is that too early for you?" Bethany couldn't help a grin as she replied in the negative. "I'll take you for a quick tour of the city before you meet our president and officers at our office. Then, we'll go to lunch and you'll make your wonderful speech on dogsled racing."

After hanging up from talking to Faye Contras, Bethany wondered what to do. Dinner? But she had eaten on the plane and wasn't hungry at all. The smart thing would be to go to bed and rest, but she did not feel tired. In fact, her muscles felt cramped and stiff from the long plane ride. She went to the window and looked out again at the brightly lit city. Surely, she could go for a walk. It seemed foolish to skulk in her hotel room. She'd be safe, she was sure; she wasn't as naive as Griff thought her to be.

At that moment, there was a knock on the door. Bethany was aware of the quick rush of excitement, the surge of happiness that inundated reason. Griff? she wondered. But when she opened the door, it was the pleasant-faced Hal Bluett.

He smiled at her surprised greeting. "Have you finished your business with the Sportswomen's Association?" She nodded, and he then said, "I hope you're not feeling too tired. My wife and I would very much enjoy your company this evening."

"Oh," she said, and then realizing how inane that response was, added, "I'm sorry. I thought that you'd be deep into that business meeting."

He shrugged ruefully. "My presence is superfluous at this stage of the game. Besides, Griff's a much tougher negotiator than I am." There was both affection and admiration in his voice, and he added, "I hope you'll come out with us. Maria is counting on it. We'll see a play first, and then get some supper. It will be a pleasure to show off New York, though after the great northern plains we'll probably come off a very poor second."

There was no doubt in her mind that Griff had arranged this outing, but for once she was grateful for his high-handedness. The Bluetts seemed genuinely pleased with her company, and she warmed immediately to Maria Bluett, a small, silver-haired woman whose commonsensical personality somehow reminded her of Julie. The play was good, and later they stopped at Mama Leone's. The huge, sprawling

building with its many lights was cheerful, and
Bethany's earlier sense of isolation completely disappeared as she chatted with the Bluetts.

Maria drew out photos of married children and a
grandchild, and initiated a lively discussion of
Bethany's life at Lover's Run. "It sounds romantic,"
she mused, "but I imagine survival out there is
hardly romantic. Dogsled racing can be dangerous,
can't it?"

She cocked her small head to one side, and
Bethany noted her concern. "Yes," she said, honestly, "There's an element of danger in racing. Danger and keen competition."

Hal shrugged ruefully. "We knew that, Maria. Griff
wouldn't go in for anything tame." He turned to
Bethany, explaining. "Griff works so darn hard at
Deane that he turns to challenge and danger as a sort
of safety valve. Perhaps you've noticed that about his
character."

She nodded. "I have indeed."

"It's the way Griff's made. His father began the
business, you know, but it's entirely due to Griff
that Deane holds an unbroken record of increased
profits and dividends. Under his leadership we've
developed overseas markets—perhaps you know
that we're hoping to expand the firm to Anchorage
soon. Then, too, he's seen that the firm expands its
interests."

Again she noted affection in his voice. "You've
known Griff a long time?" she asked.

Before Hal could reply, Maria nodded. "Ever since
he was a baby. His mother was a good friend, and
when she passed away Griff became very dear to me.
He knows how devoted Hal and I are to him, and he
cares for us also—in his own way."

Bethany raised questioning eyebrows and saw Hal
Bluett shift uneasily, saw also the warning look he

gave his wife. Maria ignored it. "Perhaps he's told you about his father?" she began. "He was a brilliant man but rather cold and aloof. Griff was taught that it was unmanly to show emotion. Fortunately, he's much more like his mother and can be capable of great sweetness."

"It's getting late." Hal glanced casually at his watch. "Bethany has to make a speech tomorrow and needs her rest." He smiled and added, "Of course, I know it's going to be a superb speech."

"You don't know anything of the kind. How could you?" She laughed and then was surprised at Hal's level look.

"I trust Griff's instincts. If you're his partner in the wilderness, I know you're an expert at what you do."

When the Bluetts had driven her back to the Centre, Bethany was in a thoughtful mood. What Maria had said about Griff gave no new insight into his character but confirmed what she'd already known. The surprise had come from the genuine affection, the tremendous respect Griff elicited from Hal. She touched the UP button of the elevator and frowned as a familiar, green-eyed face superimposed itself on the bland steel door. Everyone who knew Griff seemed to succumb to his personality and like or love him. And I? she wondered. How do I feel about him?

The elevator door opened before her, and she found herself looking directly at Griff. She had been thinking of him so intently that at first she was not surprised to see him there. "You're home already?" he exclaimed. "Weren't you out with the Bluetts?"

"I was, and they were very kind. But it's not 'already,' Griff. It's one in the morning. If you think that's early, I'm still on wilderness time."

"So late?" He held the elevator door open for her. "I was going to get a drink, but I think you're right;

I'm on wilderness time, too, and might as well get some rest." He was not standing particularly close to her in the elevator, but now as always she felt the lean power of him as palpably as she might feel his touch. "I'm sorry I wasn't able to show you the town tonight."

"No apology necessary. We both came on business, remember?"

"Oh, I remember." His mouth curved into a smile as he added, "Hopefully you also remember that saying about all work and no play making a dull human being. I think it applies to corporate heads who have to attend meetings at all hours and dogsled racers, too. Tomorrow night there's going to be a reception in one of the suites here at the complex. It's being given for me by the Halstead people. I hope you'll be my guest."

She looked ruefully down at her dress. "I'm not sure. I only brought this one dress with me."

"Very sensible. Nobody can wear two dresses at the same time." His smile lost its wry curve and became almost tender. She was reminded of what Maria Bluett had said about Griff's sweetness, and a warning whisper awoke in her mind. Don't go, Bethany. Refuse. You'll make a fool of yourself at his reception. You came here to talk at the Sportswomen's Association, not hang around Griff . . .

"I should have said, 'please' be my guest," Griff was saying. He reached out and took her hand, held it gently in his. "I guarantee that you will be the most beautiful woman there, my Beth."

She caught her breath at the familiar nickname, felt it fill her being, carry her away as he raised the hand to his lips. Warm, remembered lips touched her knuckles, then turned the hand and kissed the palm.

"I—" she stopped short as the elevator jolted to a stop and the door sighed open. It was her floor. Two people, waiting to get on, looked at her curiously. "I'll think about it," she managed.

"That's what you said when I suggested you come to New York." Quickly, she drew her hand away, but she carried the warmth of his hand, his mouth, with it. "I'll pick you up at your room at six-thirty," he added, as the elevator closed and separated them. The last thing she saw before the steel doors closed was the certainty in his eyes. How sure was he of her? Surer than she was of herself!

She had thought that she would have a hard time getting to sleep, but thankfully she found she was wrong. She even slept till eight, later than she had ever slept—or almost. Quickly she banished that morning following Katiktok's illness and hurried through the routine of bathing and dressing.

She was grateful for her long sleep, for the day proved more difficult than any run on the trails. Faye Contras picked her up punctually, and then took her on a long and often harrowing drive through the city. Later came a rather stilted meeting with the association's officers and then the luncheon itself. The speechmaking was not bad, and she truly enjoyed the question-and-answer session afterward, but by the time it was all over she was exhausted. At the hotel all she wanted to do was fall asleep.

It's dealing with all these people at once, she thought, as she put her well-earned honorarium into her purse. How did Griff do it so easily? And then, she sighed, Griff was picking her up in a half-hour's time, and it was no time to think of napping.

She compensated by taking a long bath—civilization and big cities had their very obvious advantages—then put on her dress. Last night she had dressed for her outing with the Bluetts quickly and efficiently. Tonight, she looked at herself in the full-length mirror and found she was dissatisfied. Though the cut of her dress was good, molding her slender, high-breasted figure, it lacked a certain dash. And though she had loved the color of it when she bought it long ago, the cool blue that shimmered in an Alaskan twilight, she wondered if it were sophisticated enough for Griff's reception. After all, she thought, the Halstead people are giving it in his honor. They'll know I'm his racing partner. Then she frowned. Since when had she worried what Griff's business associates might think of her?

She began to clasp a slender silver chain about her neck, but before she could fasten the catch there was a knock on the door. Still fumbling with the clasp, she went to answer it. "I'm almost ready," she told Griff, who stood outside in a dark, finely cut wool suit, a small box tucked under his arm.

"Let me help." He turned her slightly so that he could fasten the chain. For an instant, his hands rested on her shoulders, and then he said, "I think I told you before that you'd be the most dazzling woman there." As if it were the most natural thing in the world, he kissed her cheek, his roughness brushing gently against her smooth skin. Then, he placed the little box in her hands. "I hope the colors will match," he said.

The orchids in the box were a blue that almost completely blended with her dress. She had never seen such colors in a flower before, and when she placed them against her red-gold hair, she suddenly felt unique and rather beautiful. "Griff, how lovely! You have a wonderful eye for color," she cried.

"Lovely indeed." She realized that he was looking at her and not the flower, and she felt a flurry of emotions as confused and as confusing as the delicate interplay of northern lights. She looked at him uncertainly.

"Shall we go?" He was still smiling, but his voice was cool and casually friendly. "We'll take the elevator up to the suite where the reception is being held." He held out a crooked arm, and she let her fingers rest against it. Under the handsomely tailored sleeve, his muscles bunched restlessly.

"Did business go well for you?" she asked, trying to ignore the quiver of response his nearness could produce in her.

"Everything went as I'd planned. Halstead will soon become a part of my firm." Momentarily, his eyes registered satisfaction, and then he said, "How was the speech?"

He listened interestedly as she described the speech and its reception, and he asked questions that kept her talking as they rode the elevator to the reception suite. She told him about the questions that had been asked her, the people she had met. "There were some very interesting people, Griff. One woman told me that she raises Alaskan huskies in New Hampshire, not far from where I grew up. Talking with her made me feel quite nostalgic."

He raised eyebrows. "Is your stay in the Big Apple converting you to a citified way of life?" he asked, and then, more seriously, "Have you ever thought of that—leaving Lover's Run to raise your dogs elsewhere?"

She hesitated, then nodded. "Sometimes, yes. But not for very long. I love Lover's Run and my life there, as you know. Why should I give it up?"

"Why indeed." His tone was pleasant, but she felt the tightening of the arm under her hand. She looked up and saw that his attention had shifted from her as the elevator door slid open. "Here we are," he told her.

Griff's party was being held in a large suite, and the room was filled with people. Her eyes registered a dazzle of well-dressed women, men in dark business attire, a lavish table spread with food and drink. She also noted that interested eyes were on her, some curious, some speculative, some amused. They were all conjecturing on Griff's latest girlfriend, she thought, and was surprised at the small spurt of defensiveness within her. Why shouldn't they wonder? she asked herself. She had, after all, come in with the guest of honor.

"Bethany, how nice you look." Maria Bluett was at her side, an arm around her waist. She stood on tiptoe to kiss Griff's cheek and added, "I suppose you men are going to talk boring business, so I'll spirit Bethany away."

Griff had no time to reply. His name was being called, his hand shaken, and he was already surrounded by half a dozen men and women. Over the heads of this small crowd he sent Bethany and Maria an apologetic glance.

"You mustn't mind," Maria said. She began to lead Bethany further into the suite. "Griff's going to have to make polite business talk for a while: it's expected. I used to loathe it when Hal brought me to these affairs, but they're a fact of life and you get used to them."

Bethany wondered if she ever could get used to the talk and the noise. At the same time she was determined to store up as many reminiscences as possible to tell the Kobuks later. She smiled at Maria. "Thank you for coming to my rescue," she said. "I'd love to meet some of your friends."

"Ammunition first." Maria scooped two glasses of wine from a passing waitress, handed one to Bethany, and raised the glass. "These people aren't exactly friends, Bethany, more like important business associates of Hal and Griff. But you'll see. Just smile and be your charming self."

She did her best, but before long she was wondering why she had come. Though the people Maria introduced her to seemed pleasant, none of them had much interest in her beyond the fact that she was Griff's partner in dogsled racing.

"Have you known Griff long?" one woman asked. Then, on being told of Lover's Run, she looked astonished. "You don't mean to tell me you live out there with the Eskimos? You have a house, don't you, not an igloo?"

"Eskimos don't live in igloos—" but the woman had lost interest and was talking about the latest broadway play with Maria. Sighing, Bethany sipped her wine. She now knew why Maria had called it ammunition.

When Maria finally extricated herself, she rolled her eyes. "Takes all types, you know." Suddenly, she winced. "Oh, Lord, there's Burgess." Bethany's eyes asked a question, and she explained, "Ed Burgess. He's one of the higher-ups on the corporate scene—a big wheel in computers and software—and one of the biggest bores around. I'm afraid there's no way of avoiding him."

A small and rotund man was headed right toward them. He carried a half-empty glass in his hand, Bethany noted, and when he greeted them his voice was loud and a little slurred. "Well, the little lady from the frozen north, isn't it? I've heard all about you, dear."

Bethany tried for a polite smile, murmured a greeting. Maria made a few moments' small talk, then skillfully extricated Bethany from his presence, and eased her into a group that was discussing local politics. As the talk shifted and moved from one point to another, Bethany found her eyes straying to the corner of the room where Griff was deep in discussion with a small group of his colleagues. As if aware of her regard, he met her eyes with a quick, emerald look that made her turn quickly away. It's not anyone's fault that I'm bored here, she thought. I've just got to make the best of it. It can't last too much longer.

The discussion had heated up and was, by now, totally uninteresting. Seeing that Maria was talking as loudly and as animatedly as the rest, Bethany stepped away from the group. If nothing else, the food on the long table looked excellent. She owed the Kobuks a long description of exquisite hors d'oeuvres that didn't have moose or caribou in them. She smiled at the thought and was moving in on the table when a man's moist, warm hand caught hers.

"Wait up, darling. I do want to talk to you," Ed Burgess said.

Inwardly she groaned. The pressure of his hand was unpleasant, and so was the vaguely drunken look he turned on her. "I always wanted to talk to somebody from Alaska," he was saying. "I think it's a fascinating place. Land of perpetual dark and oil. Eh?"

Bethany looked around for Maria, but her one friend was deep in her discussion of New York politics. She sighed. "It's really not always dark there," she explained. "There's some light even in the dead of winter."

Ed Burgess obviously didn't like being contradicted. His small, puffy eyes narrowed. "Next you're going to say there's no oil there either," he quipped.

"I'm not going to say that, although oil and offshore drilling can be a curse as well as a boon." She knew as the words left her lips that this was a mistake. Burgess leaned forward.

"You're against progress—that it?" He wagged a plump finger. "You're too pretty to be so opinionated. Surely you don't want us all back in the dark ages hunting with spears?"

It was useless to argue with him. She began to head for the table again, but he followed, cataloging a list of the wonderful things that had been achieved in Alaska with the advent of oil. She kept silent as long as she could, but the wine she'd drunk earlier seemed to have gone to her head and she finally blurted, "Progress is a two-edged sword. It's also brought alcholism and unemployment to Alaska."

"If people want to drink themselves silly no one can stop them. As for unemployment, Eskimos aren't progressive, are they?"

She thought of the Kobuks and anger rose into her throat. Nevertheless she said, "That's not true. A friend of mine, an Eskimo, sent his son to a white man's high school. Now the boy can't get a job, but he can't hunt or fish in the traditional way, either."

"So you have Eskimo friends?" He slid an arm around her. "Do they really rub noses when they kiss, eh?"

"One thing about Eskimos, they have wonderful manners." Her voice shook as she pulled free from him. "Perhaps you'd be wise to learn from them."

It seemed to her as if the room had suddenly gone silent. Ed Burgess' eyes were popping out of his suddenly red face, and all at once she could stand being there no longer. Swiftly she turned and pushed her way toward the suite door, and walked through it without a backward look. She'd had enough of big-city parties and big-city manners, she thought bitterly. I've had it with all of them, she thought furiously.

Anger carried her to her room but once there, it faded into a dull, cold unhappiness. It wasn't my fault, she thought, he started it. Even Maria said he was a terrible bore. But she had been mannerless, too, walking out without a word to Maria or Griff. At the thought of Griff another wave of anger rose and mixed with the pain. He just took me there and dumped me with his so-called friends. "Go with me as my guest," he had said. Was this how big moguls treated their guests?

She paced her hotel room restlessly, hating it, hating the city, hating the scene that had just ended. Finally, knowing that she could only work off her tense unhappiness by exercise, she reached for her coat and slid it over her dress. As she reached to settle the hood of the coat about her face, she touched an unexpected, forgotten softness in her hair, and the blue orchid slid into her hands. For a moment she looked at it, and then she put it down. After tonight, the softness she'd seen in Griff's eyes as he gave her this flower would never be there again.

"What do I care?" she muttered, locking her door after her and punching the DOWN elevator button. She was not responsible to him, not answerable to him. If she was upset about the scene with Burgess, it was because she should have kept her temper.

She intended to walk for only a few blocks, but she ended up by doing a great deal more. She became lost in the maze of unfamiliar streets and traffic, lost her way in a totally new part of the city. By the time she had finally made her way back to the Centre, it was late and very cold. Nor was this the cold and dark of the wilderness, for there were few stars that could compete with the bright city lights. And instead of the clean sound of the wind, there were jumbled traffic and siren noises, as people jostled through the crowded streets. And even though there were so many people, Bethany had never felt so alone, so isolated. She was grateful to reach the hotel and her room.

But as she walked down the hallway toward the room she heard her name called. "Where in hell have you been?" Griff demanded.

She whirled to face him, shocked both by the suddenness of his appearance and the harshness of his voice. In the dim hall light he looked bigger and broader of shoulder than ever, almost menacing. He wore an overcoat over the business suit he'd worn to the reception and had obviously been out himself.

"I went for a walk," she said.

He clicked his tongue in disgust. "Didn't I tell you not to walk in this city at night? Do you think you're back in that wilderness of yours? You've been gone a good two hours, dammit. I thought you might have been mugged or gotten sick again somewhere. I was ready to call the police."

Her own surge of indignation at his manner deafened her to the real anxiety in his voice. She heard only his anger. "I'm sorry that you were concerned, but as I've said before, I can take care of myself." She walked briskly to her room, turned her key in the lock, and opened it.

The door was snatched out of her hand. "You're not just going to walk away from me. "He pushed the door open, caught her by the arm, and pushed her forward into the room, then entered it himself. He closed the door behind them both and glared at her.

"I don't recall inviting you in here," she snapped.

"You owe me an explanation. Storming out of that reception as you did was the act of a spoiled brat." Each word of his was clipped, sharpened, hurled to wound. "Maria was distraught. One minute you were with her, the next you were gone." The thought of Maria's distress made her try to explain, but he stopped her with his next words. "I know you think you're too fine to mingle with us city peasants, but that was no excuse for your rudeness."

"My rudeness!" Almost speechless, she faced him with blazing eyes. "You have absolutely no right to question me about my behavior, now or ever. I—let me go, damn you, Griff Deane. Let me go right now!"

He had caught her by the arms and now he roared down at her. "Let you go? I should. I don't know why I don't, you maddening woman! Can't you see . . ."

Griff finished the sentence in his mind, unable to say the words out loud. "Can't you see how much I was worried about you? If something worried or hurt you, couldn't you have trusted me enough to come and tell me?"

She could see, all right, Bethany thought. She read it all on his face: his disgust at her gauche manners, the disgrace she had brought him among his friends. The indignant anger she had used to shore her defenses against him suddenly collapsed into an ache that was so terrible it was almost physical. "Let me go," she repeated. He must not see her cry.

He sensed rather than heard the change in her voice, and something within him responded involuntarily. Before either of them knew how or exactly why, he had pulled her into his arms.

His lips came down on hers, hard, still-angry lips. The kiss was almost painful in its intensity, and the punishing arms held her bruisingly, almost crushing her against the rock-hard wall of his chest. She struggled to pull free from his clasp, and yet something within her was responding to the wildness of his kiss. There was something primal in his mouth, something stripped of all civilized veneer and going below the layers of sophistication to the savage emotions of the wilderness. In spite of herself, her mouth opened under his, her tongue warred with his.

He murmured something deep in his throat as his lips ravaged her mouth, savoring, demanding. His hands moved swiftly, not with learned restraint but with passion that made them fumble as he slid down

the zipper of her dress, then pushed it roughly over
her shoulders, pushed down straps and lace to cup
her bared breasts.

She felt an equal tumult within her, a tormenting
maelstrom of conflicting feelings that resulted in a
want too great to bear. She pushed at the heavy coat
he wore, and it fell onto the carpeted floor. Then the
suit coat and vest. She felt the softness of his shirt
against her breasts as he carried her to the bed, felt
the touch of material pucker her ready nipples further, further stir the erotic whirlpool within her.

In total silence she reached for the buttons of his
shirt, working buttons away from their fastenings.
Swiftly, still kissing her, he removed his clothes, her
dress, slip. Then, he claimed the warm thrust of her
breasts as if this were his right, kissing the eager nipples, raising their tormented peaks against his
demanding, drawing mouth. Then he was sliding his
thumbs under her panty hose, yanking down with a
trembling impatience equal to her own.

She wanted him so much, and yet now she hesitated. They had made love before, but not like this.
The scarcely leashed ferocity in both of them frightened her, suddenly, and she whispered the first word
she had spoken—his name—in protest. Not this way,
she wanted to cry, not like this—not in anger. She
raised her eyes to his and saw the look in them, saw
no anger but only an overwhelming need.

She lifted her arms to draw him closer and he came
to her quickly, his body urgent against hers. She felt
the hotel blankets slide against her bare back, his
flesh sweet on hers—muscle and sinew and breast-
tickling fur—imprinting her with his want of her. His
hands and mouth worked wild possession on her,
and she was making soft, wanting noises in her throat
as she opened her heart and herself to his maraud-
ing conquest.

Whose conquest? Whose victory? It did not matter. Almost mindless, now, she moved against him while seeking closeness and still more closesness. It seemed that she could not reach it, not find it, and she gasped his name and heard him murmur incoherently against her tumbled red-gold hair.

"Beth, my Beth," he whispered as the universe shattered around them. And as it did, as she shattered with it, she could hold onto only one thought and one reality. She loved this man—now and forever.

Chapter Twelve

❧

Next morning when she woke he was gone and she was alone. She lay very still in the big bed, her body curled in on itself as if conserving the energy needed to face what had happened.

It had happened. Though she had slept deeply, she had no hope that she had dreamed what had passed between herself and Griff. And if she had so deluded herself, the bed held subtle reminders of the man: his subtle scent of mingled after-shave and clean male fragrance, the indented pillow, the full, satisfied feeling of her body.

But it was false satisfaction. Face it now, face it forever, she told herself firmly. He came to me because he was angry at me. No matter what he might have felt later, no matter what I felt . . .

She felt it now, the keen, soaring pleasure, the ripples of wanting that had exploded the earth and the sky. For a moment she held the memory, and then let it go. I must let it all go, she thought, and was suddenly frightened because she didn't know whether she could.

She kept herself busy that morning. There was another, smaller meeting with the Sportswomen's Association, lunch with Faye Contras. In the afternoon, she took a sightseeing bus and toured the city's attractions, then shopped for souvenirs for the Kobuk family. She stayed out as long as she decently could before she returned to the Centre. There were two messages for her. One was from Maria, inviting her to dinner. The other was from Griff.

She opened the note with decisive fingers that hid an inner trembling. She read the terse, scant writing in the bold hand. "Business will keep me occupied this evening and tomorrow morning. Hope to leave for Anchorage on the earliest plane and will advise you." The stilted, formal language of the business world prodded through her hastily erected defenses, and she bit her lip as he concluded, "I'm sorry about the reception and the *contretemps*."

Contretemps. She tried the word softly as she rode the elevator up to her room, then laughed at herself for caring what he called what had happened. My fault, she thought, all my fault. I knew from the first moment I saw him he'd be trouble. She felt sudden tears dart to her eyes and wiped them swiftly and impatiently away with the backs of her hands. He might be trouble, but he was still her partner until the Rohn Relay. Until that happened—and thankfully, it wasn't so far away—she'd make darn sure that no further *contretemps* occurred between them.

Their return flight to Anchorage was smooth and mostly silent. Griff was absorbed in a briefcase full of paperwork, and Bethany pretended interest in a slick magazine Maria Bluett had thrust, along with a little gift, into her hands. The sophisticated, bold photographs of professional models danced from the printed page to her eye and reminded her of the well-dressed folk at the reception. Eventually, she put the magazine down and prayed that she could soon be home in Lover's Run.

Once in Anchorage, she felt better. But when they had boarded the Aztec plane that would bring them to Raedar, she did not feel the hoped-for surge of joy.

The view of the country she loved, dark tundra and forest, sparkling lakes and stern mountains washed by scudding clouds, did not excite her or welcome her as they should. To her disappointment the emptiness within her remained hollow, disquieting, as if her brief visit to New York had changed her in some unknown way. I'm home, she kept telling herself, but the interior vacuum persisted. Only when they reached Raedar and were met by the entire clan of Kobuks did her depression ease.

"That's what I call a hug," Julie said comfortably, as Bethany wrapped her arms around her. "Let me look at you. She took the Big Apple by storm, huh, Griff?"

"By storm," he agreed, but both his voice and eyes were unreadable. And then he said, "It's been a long trip, folks. I don't know about Bethany, but I'm ready to sleep for a few days."

"Whooping it up in the city." Elmer's voice had a touch of envy. "Tell you what, Griff. You go straight home with the others, and Tony or me will take Bethany home."

Griff did not protest. She realized that he no more relished the thought of being alone with her than she did with him, and she was grateful for Elmer's suggestion. Yet, there was a small nub of hurt within her as Tony eagerly volunteered his services.

"I can tell Bethany how well the dogs are doing," he explained.

"Yes, the dogs." Griff looked straight at Bethany. "Do you feel strong enough to begin training again, Bethany? Or would you like a few days' rest after the trip?"

"No, I'd like to start." Unflinchingly, she met his look. He must never know how she felt, what she felt. To him I am just a contretemps, she reminded herself, as she added aloud, "New York was fine to visit but I'm very grateful to be home and doing things I care about again."

At the cabin the dogs gave her an ecstatic greeting, and the familiar peace of the wilderness soothed her. Yet later that night she started awake hearing the wind sing outside the wooden walls, and she thought of the incessant noises and sirens of New York and of Talka hunting for her lover. There's loneliness everywhere, she thought, listening to the swell of the wind. She must admit it, conquer it, and go on.

Outwardly she had completely conquered her feelings. By morning, she had slid back into the old routine of her days. Before Griff arrived, water had been drawn, dogs fed, sleds readied. And when they raced, she found that her stamina and strength had returned so that she could often outmaneuver, outrace him. When they tried the exercises Griff had invented to train for the relay, her time was better than his.

"New York seems to have agreed with you," he said, and she smiled at him.

"You pick up a lot of useful knowledge wherever you go," she told him easily.

But there was no real ease between them. The first day's running was marred because of this and the subsequent days were no better. There was a tension; not the old tension of attraction that had drawn them together even as they fought against it, but a silence that seemed to grow and widen between them. It cut into the intuitive support they had given each other, and the competition between them now had a cutting edge. Once, when Griff had bested her in time, Bethany felt a spurt of anger. He seemed to sense it and said, "I told you that I'd beat you one day, and I will. As soon as we're no longer partners—partner."

"That will be the day!" she snapped back. "You can't have your way in everything, Griff Deane."

"You think so?" His green eyes blazed momentarily, then became hard as he turned away from her. "We'll see about that as soon as the Rohn is over."

Were they partners or combatants? Bethany didn't know anymore. As the days passed and the Rohn drew closer she wondered. Sometimes she was so fed up with the tension between them that she wanted to shout at Griff, tell him that she was breaking their association. But the angry spirit of competition between them wouldn't let her give in. Let him be the first to cry uncle, she thought grimly. Surely he wasn't enjoying things any more than she was.

Apparently, he wasn't, though he wasn't the one to tell her so. Julie Kobuk and Giuliana stopped by Bethany's cabin one afternoon to visit and help sew the innumerable dog booties that would soon be needed. As they sat by the wood stove, Julie broached the subject in an uncharacteristically hesitant way.

"Anything—ah—happen in New York?" she began.

Bethany was surprised. "Of course, a lot of things happened. I made my speech, met a lot of people—"

"I didn't mean that." Julie stabbed a needle through the leather bootie in her hand. "You and Griff came back sort of different." Bethany said nothing, and the big woman sighed. "So I'm a nosy old lady who cares about you, Bethy. I know you, and I can see you're not happy. Neither is Griff. He used to talk a lot about your racing, what you two did, but now he's silent."

"Perhaps he wants out of the partnership," Bethany said. She got up, walked to the stove, and set a kettle on for tea.

"Perhaps he does," Julie said softly.

"Has he said so?" But Julie was shaking her head. "Why do you say so, then? It's nothing to keep secret.

If he wants to break the partnership, all he has to do is tell me."

Her voice trembled involuntarily on the last words, and she unconsciously straightened her spine, lifted her chin. This had gone far enough. Tomorrow, she thought, I'll tell Griff that if he wants out it's okay with me.

True to her resolve, she brought up the subject as they were harnessing the dogs in the dusky early morning. "I need to talk to you," she told him, without preamble. "I think it's time we discussed the Rohn and our partnership."

"Do you?" If he knew what she was after, he certainly wasn't about to help her. Bethany frowned as he added, "Well, then, talk away, partner. I'm sure you have something interesting to say."

"I've been feeling a tension between us." Drawing a deep breath she faced him. His eyes were hard and still, watchful under the headlamp strapped to his forehead. "It's not too late to find another partner, if necessary. There are still some weeks until the Rohn."

"If that's what you want." Abruptly, he swung his long legs into the sled, called to his dogs, and flicked the reins. She watched him drive away from her and bit her lip. What *she* wanted? Why couldn't the man stay and discuss what *he* wanted? Irritably, she climbed into her sled and followed him. Whether he liked it or not, there was need of further talk about this.

He gave her no chance to talk further. Today he seemed set on bettering his recorded time, set on pushing himself and his team to their fullest limits. Grimly determining not to be bested, Bethany kept pace with him. When they at last halted, the teams were running neck and neck.

"I congratulate you." The morning's brusqueness

had faded from his voice and he sounded more like his old self—weary but pleased. "You're a good driver, Bethany Sheridan." And then he added, "If I do beat you, it'll be because of the things you taught me."

There was something in his voice that made her realize that this was the moment of severance, of breaking the partnership. Instead of a relief she felt a sharp pang. It was almost better to part on a note of anger than with grateful politeness. She raised her head and met his gaze full on.

"If you beat me it won't be for my lack of trying," she told him. "You're a fine racer, Griff, but I'm good, too. As I said, we've still got time to find partners and register in the Rohn as separate teams."

His teeth gleamed in an unlooked-for smile. "Maybe you're right. But for now—how about a private race back to your cabin? A race of time. We'll synchronize our watches and see who's really the best at this game."

So the big mogul was making his last bid to win over her, conquer her. Nodding briskly, she accepted the challenge. "We'll take the same route we ordinarily take. It's a forty-mile run, Griff." Even now she couldn't help herself from adding, "Be careful."

He did not hear her. She saw tension in the way he took the reins, bent over them. Then, both of them were on their way. "Gee," Bethany heard Griff command his dogs. "Gee, good dogs!"

They started neck and neck, then surged back and forth—Griff leading first, falling back behind Bethany, moving forward again. She wondered if she could beat him. He was too swift, too good a racer. She tried every trick she knew to get back the lead, got it, and then had him overtake her. Well, the race was far from over. There were miles and miles ahead of them. She would let him think he was gaining, and then . . .

Some sixth sense made her look up without finishing her thought. For a moment she sensed rather than saw it, and then the big-antlered shadow was moving fast, speeding toward them with a click-click-click of sound. It came over a hummock of earth and snow and blundered directly into the path of Griff's sled.

"Griff!" she yelled. "Look out! Moose! Bear left, Griff. *Haw* . . ."

She didn't know whether he'd heard her or seen the beast himself, but she saw his swift reaction as he turned his sled to the left. She screamed to her own dogs, struggling to pull them to a stop, throwing every ounce of her strength into controlling the madly bucking sled. Then, she was sweeping by Griff, and as she did so she heard the thud of a heavy body hitting the sled, the yowling of angry, frightened dogs.

She swiveled her head to see. The moose was loping off, Griff's sled upended in the sparse snow. Dogs were tangled in their tethers, but she could not see Griff. She shouted his name and heard no answer.

She finally managed to stop her dogs, anchor the sled to the ground. Then, snow creaking under her in her hurry, she raced back to Griff's sled. Dimly, she registered that the sled had been damaged by the moose's heavy hoofs. "Griff?" she shouted again. "Where are you?"

She saw him then, a dark curl on the white snow. Her heart stopped, her breathing stilled, the blood in her froze over. Griff lay so still, arms flung out, legs under him. Oh, my God, she thought, and a terror so vast and chill she could not cope with it gripped her. She thought, I'm going to pass out, and then she forced herself forward. What good would she be to him if she fainted?

She knelt on the snow beside him and felt for a pulse. For a moment she could not find it, and she pressed her ear to his chest. To her intense relief his chest rose and fell steadily; his heartbeat was strong. Alive, her heart sang and blood and breath moved again. But how badly was he hurt? There was a bruise on his forehead, a gash on his cheek. She'd need to get him to the cabin to take care of him better. She looked over her shoulder. First, she'd have to get him to the sled.

Her knees buckled as she went to collect her dogs and bring them nearer. Then she knelt down again and put her arms around him. He was a big man, heavy, but she'd manage.

"This is pleasant. Almost worth a brush with a moose to get treatment like this."

Griff's eyes were open and looking up into hers. She could only blink at first, and then a huge relief dazed her eyes with tears. "Are you hurt? was all she could say. "Did it hurt you?"

"I was thrown when it hit the sled. Going the speed I was, I'd hate to think of the impact with which I hit the ground, but I've got a hard head." His eyes smiled up at her.

She realized that she was still holding him close to her and that his dark, hatless head was pressing against her. She helped him sit up, thus removing him from such personal contact. "I tried to warn you."

"I heard you." He pressed a hand to his temple and, worried, she supported him again as he said, "I think your warning may have saved my hide, Beth. I was so hell-bent on beating you that I never heard or saw the brute till too late." He paused. "You knew I wanted to beat you?"

"Yes," she said impatiently. "That doesn't matter now."

"But it does." He turned swiftly, the green of his eyes intense in the Arctic dark. "It matters more than anything else. You matter, Beth."

She knew that she was looking at him with her heart in her eyes.

He saw it, too, the softness, the tenderness he had fought so long against, had so long wanted. From the depth of his heart he whispered, "Oh, my love," and drew her close into his arms.

She nestled against him as if this was the only sane and right action in the universe. She felt him kiss her tumbled hair and heard his voice, ragged, shorn of anything but honesty. "I'm in love with you," he was saying. "I love you, Beth."

She heard the words with mind and heart. She wanted to, but could not answer. In mute wonder she clung to him as he said, "I tried not to love you. I needed you so much, and I was afraid of that need. I tried to put you at arm's length and couldn't. I tried to leave you alone and couldn't. I even tried to drive you away from me—and could do nothing but love you more."

She lifted her face and he kissed her: her mouth, her cold cheeks with the salt of her tears on them. Tears she had shed for him, he thought, and something in his tight chest yielded and loosened so that he felt the first ripples of a surprising joy. "I thought you hated me," she was whispering. "I thought you were disgusted by what I did in New York."

"You didn't do anything at all in New York." His arms tightened around her. "When I took you with me, I wasn't really thinking of you. I was being selfish. I wanted you close to me, wanted to show you off as my partner even though I wouldn't admit I needed you around me. At that reception I should have stayed with you, instead of which I left you to the mercies of Ed Burgess." He grinned suddenly. "You certainly did tell him off, my love. It'll be some time before he accosts another pretty woman at a party." The grin faded then, and he added, "I was sure you loathed me for putting you in that position. And later, I was very angry with you. So angry I forgot my promises to leave you alone."

"Griff, you're usually so smart," she sighed. "Couldn't you see me wanting and loving you? How could you believe anything else?"

For a long time they knelt together, kissing, holding, whispering. Then Freya whined and Katiktok gave a sharp, impatient bark. Griff drew slowly away from Bethany. "I think it's time we went home."

Their sense of partnership seemed reborn. They attached Griff's damaged sled to Bethany's, gathered up the dogs, and rode back slowly to Lover's Run. They did not kiss or talk as they went about the chores of feeding dogs and caring for them, but she could feel without touch or word or even look, the sweet, steady flow of electricity between them, a warmth as vital to her as the flow of blood.

Later, he put his arms around her waist as they went to the cabin together, and he kissed her as they stepped through the door. It seemed as if the dark warmth of the cabin welcomed them home.

Oddly, there was no hurry. Though their want of each other was almost overwhelming, it did not consume them or cause them to neglect what was needed. Bethany heated water to tend Griff's cuts, carefully cleaning the dirt mixed with blood on his forehead and cheek. As she worked, they stopped to kiss, whispering together. I've missed you—and I thought of you so much—I've wanted to love you.

They undressed eath other leisurely by the light of a single lamp, helping with buttons and unwieldy northern clothing, reaching the beloved flesh below. Bethany kissed the darkening bruise against Griff's shoulder, another on his thigh. He trembled as his mouth found familiar sweetness at her breast, her mouth.

"I've wanted to do this, and this," he breathed against her, and she fitted herself against him, murmuring her love. The words rose gladly in them as if, long dammed like winter ice, they were glad to thaw into spring warmth.

Even when he carried her to the bed they did not hurry. Though fire swept through them in floods, they whispered and kissed and paused to caress. And at last when they lost themselves in the sweet swirl of senses that could no longer be put off or delayed, there was a difference, too. Though the satin of her body's warmth, his hard passion, were the same, they had changed. As she took him deep within her, she took his love. The sweetness of her movements that roared through him in passion and tenderness was love. Smiling at each other, whispering love words centuries new, they melded into one song of love and desire and complete trust. Truly one.

Chapter Thirteen

Little ripples of pleasure still caressed her as she came awake. She heard the wind's calling outside, Talka looking for Nowak, and somehow tonight the noise was far more poignant than ever before. As this thought touched her mind she heard his voice.

"I think even the Lovers have found each other tonight. The wind seems happy."

His voice did not come from close beside her, and she propped herself up on her elbow to look. He was not in bed, but she could see the broad-shouldered shadow of him by the window. He'd thrown a blanket about him and he seemed wrapped in darkness.

"What are you looking at?" she asked softly, and he held out a hand to her.

"Watching the northern lights. Come and look at them with me, Beth."

She went to him quickly, her flesh goose pimpling against the cool of the cabin. Then she was warm again as he pulled her back into his arms so that her bare back rested against his chest. He covered them both with the blanket, wrapping his arms around her waist under her breasts.

"Is that better?" he murmured, and she turned to rub her cheek against his. The sensuous warmth of his flesh against hers, the rasp of the blanket on her soft skin, excited her. But together with the excitement came the same sure delight that they had found together yesterday in their lovemaking and the long talking between the loving. It was a feeling of true completion, of separateness made whole. She sighed her satisfaction as he kissed her, his mouth moving over hers with great tenderness.

"I've watched the lights many times from the Kobuks' house. I always thought of you when they came and went, and I wanted you desperately. Many times I had to stop myself from coming over here to you."

She leaned back against his hard shoulder and saw the swirling of lights against the sky. Brilliant sashes of green and gold, the strange lights undulated against the darkness. Sharp one moment, soft and elusive the next, they slipped and eddied and moved in celestial dance.

"I've never seen them so lovely," she said softly, and he touched her neck and shoulder with small kisses.

"Even the gods are glad that you're with me at last." He sounded contented, the happiness in him running as deep as hers. His arms tightened around her. "This is really all that matters, isn't it?"

For answer she turned so that she faced him and put her arms around his neck, drawing his dark head down to meet her upraised one. "I love you," she whispered against his lips, the words dancing like small kisses between them.

"I adore you." She couldn't get enough of hearing those words from him, and she made a sound of satisfaction that was almost a deep-throated purr. "You're mine, Beth. I should have scooped you up and carried you away that first day I met you. I'd come looking for a partner for the Rohn event, but the moment I saw you nothing was of any importance anymore."

"And now?" she asked. "What is important now?"

She had meant it lightly, a form of loving teasing, but while she said the words she noted that often-seen shadowing of his expressive eyes. "Now," he said, and his voice was thoughtful, the voice she had heard in New York when he discussed business with Hal Bluett. "We've got to think about 'now' together, Beth. We'll work it out."

She wished she had never asked the question, for she knew how he had interpreted it. Though they loved each other, the differences that had separated them before were still there, still wedged deep in their lives. Something restless shifted in her brain as she thought that in all their loving and during the sweet, drowsy talk that followed, they had not talked of their future beyond the Rohn Relay.

"I don't want to talk just now," he was whispering. His kisses had become more intense, and she turned to them and him and gladly let the troublesome thoughts go. As he said, they would work things out. Their love was so new, too new to spoil with plans and long discussions. She felt the soft prickle of chest fur against her smooth breasts, his hard body against her softness. "Hold me," she whispered.

"Always." His mouth claimed hers, and the blanket slipped from around them, fell to the floor. She shivered against the sudden intrusion of cool air, and he whispered, "You're cold. I know a way to warm you, love."

How many ways were there to love a man? she wondered. It seemed that if she and Griff loved until forever, the moments of shared desire would always change, revealing another facet of passion, new depths of love. Last night they loved with laughter, even with teasing as they learned new ways to pleasure one another. This morning's lovemaking was different still, almost recalling the wild, soul-shattering coming together in New York. There was an edge of the primal in the way Griff kissed her mouth and breasts and hands, in the way he mapped her body with his hands and mouth, seeking out all the small, sensitive parts of her until there were no secrets, no mysteries left.

"I love you," he whispered, when he finally came to her, "I adore you." She heard the huskiness in his deep voice, gloried in the tremble of his strong-muscled body, loved him so much that she strove to give him more and yet more, taking him deep and even deeper within her, surrendering her soul and her heart to him while yet holding him willing prisoner. And as they caught flame together, burned as bright as the glorious northern lights together, she called his name. My love, my love—over and over until she lay still in his arms.

Later, they heated the sauna stones and bathed together, and then went about the chores of the day as they had many times before. But there was a difference in everything today, and Griff put this into words as they walked together to the frozen lake for water.

"I feel that whatever I do today is a little like making love to you," he said.

His tone carried a note of wonder, and she knew suddenly and completely how many were the ways of loving. As long as she and Griff lived, there would be a renewal of love in the simplest things: a look, a touch, shared tasks, whispered encouragement. So much comprised love beyond the physical bonding, and she drew in the clean, sharp northern cold and wondered at it all. She tried to explain what she felt to Griff, and he slid an arm around her and held her close.

"I know. I've felt that way, too," he sighed. "It seems all so simple and clear now . . ."

His words trailed away, and again, as she had felt

back at the cabin, Bethany felt a stir of uneasiness. He was thinking of his corporation again, his role in another world. Carefully she said, "but there are times when it isn't so clear?"

He did not answer, and she sensed he was frowning. They were silent as they got the water, and they were on their way back to the hut when he spoke again. "Beth, I love you very much. You know that. And I need you—no matter what else, that remains unchanged. But neither of us is a child, and we know that life is made of other factors besides loving. We'll both have to make adjustments in our way of life."

She frowned as she thought of New York and Ed Burgess. She could never "adjust" to that milieu. "I don't think I can ever live in a big city," she began slowly. "I want to be as honest as I can, Griff."

He squeezed her hand. "We needn't live in a big city. There are suburbs, rural areas. Remember that woman you met from the Sportswomen's Association who raised dogs in New Hampshire?"

She hesitated. Could she leave the silences and the brave independence of Lover's Run? She thought of the dark winters when her dogs raced, their breaths frozen on their muzzles. She thought of the summers that splashed the earth with ferns and grasses and the Alaskan cotton grass that jockeyed with berry bushes and birch and spurce and alder. Could she really give all this up? she wondered.

As if he read her thoughts, he bent and kissed her forehead, his lips warm on her cold skin. "We'll have to go slowly and carefully, Beth. We'll work something out between us. The important thing is that we love each other." He paused and added quietly, "When we're married we'll decide what next to do."

She stopped in her tracks and stared up at him. His proud dark head was etched against the northern lights, his face shadowed in the darkness. "What did you say?"

"You heard exactly what I said. Of course we're marrying. I'm not the kind of man to engage in a casual affair with—stop it, my love." He laughed as she hit him on the shoulder. "You'll spill the water. Don't you want to make an honest man of me?"

"I doubt I could. You're devious, Griff Deane!" He set the water bucket down and gathered her into his arms, and she added, "Did I say I'd marry you?"

His smile was both wicked and tender. "No—you showed me. Last night and this morning." His lips were sweet on hers. "Bethany Deane. Has a nice ring to it, don't you think? If you like, we can be married in Raedar. They have a church there, and Giuliana would be an enchanting flower girl."

Half laughing, half exasperated, she shook her head at him. It was like him to make all the decisions, she thought. "But we need to talk about important things," she told him. Her words became increasingly garbled through his kisses. "Griff, please. Where would we live? We have to—Griff, stop it!"

"You don't want me to stop," he told her, and he was right. Already her blood was warming to his nearness, his kisses. "I adore you," he whispered, as he picked her up and carried her the last few yards to the cabin. "We'll be happy, my Beth—trust me." And in his arms again, warmed by his body and his love, she did.

Later, they drove into Tilikit together, and while Griff went to take his sled for repair, Bethany stopped in to visit Julie. The big woman was sewing this morning, her lap covered with bright cloth. "It's a dress," she explained. "Elmer surprised me by bringing home a dress length for Giuliana and me. I told him that the only time I'd maybe need a new dress was for a wedding."

Bethany's mouth kept pulling into a smile. Now, she grinned at her friend's shrewd black eyes. "So maybe there will be a wedding," she said.

Julie leaned forward. "You got any idea who might be getting married?" she demanded. Then, as Bethany's face gave her feelings away, she let out a whoop and jumped up to hug her. "Didn't I tell you? And here you were talking about splitting up your partnership for the Rohn event." She paused. "You still going to run in that? I'm glad. I don't want to lose you any faster than I have to."

"You won't lose me," Bethany said, laughing.

Julie sighed. "Of course not, Bethy. It's just that it's been fun to have you within visiting distance. But I guess Griff will surely bring you back to visit often, won't he?"

"Bring me back from where? We haven't decided where to live yet, Julie." She wished that Julie had not brought up the subject, for she had managed to quiet her uneasiness in Griff's arms, and now it sprang forward again. Julie was shaking her head.

"Woman goes where her husband goes," she said. "Even Talka, strong as she was, came with Nonak to Lover's Run. When I married Elmer, I left my home to go with him. The good book says it too, Bethy. 'Whither thou goest, I will go.' " Bethany said nothing and Julie added softly, "I know living here means a lot to you, but think of what Griff's world means to him. He built up his corporation and made it run so big and fine. Men need their business and their work, honey. We women are smarter. All we need is love."

"I don't agree with you," Bethany said stubbornly. Yet, balanced against Griff's corporation and its enormous tallies of profits and power, her world seemed small indeed.

Julie lifted a warning finger. "If you remember, Bethy, all this happened one time before—with

Piers. You didn't want to leave your way of living or Lover's Run for him, and yet you missed him, didn't you? And you didn't care for Piers like you love Griff."

Before Bethany could reply, the Kobuks' front door swung open and Griff came in. He answered Julie's sallies and congratulations by swinging her off her feet in a bear hug, but even as he smiled, Bethany realized that he was preoccupied.

"Is the sled badly damaged?" she asked.

"No. They can repair it in a day or so." He hesitated, then came to her and took both her hands. "I'd hoped to go back to Lover's Run with you, but I'm afraid something's come up. While I was seeing about that sled, I got word that there's a special message for me at Raedar. Our man in Anchorage has some urgent word from Hal Bluett. I have to go to Raedar right away and see what's going on."

"Can I come with you?" she asked. Again he hesitated, then shook his head.

"I don't think it will be wise, love. I may be tied up for some time." He paused. "Let Tony or Elmer take you home, all right? I'll be back with you as soon as I can."

She kissed him, wondering if he knew that his voice had changed, that the look in his eyes was subtly different. It was as if he weren't seeing her as much as the problem waiting for him, as if he were not looking forward so much to her and Lover's Run as he was to the challenge of cleaning up some business contretemps. The word brushed up against her mind, disturbing her in spite of herself. Swiftly she pushed it away. She must not be petty. As Julie said, Griff's business was of great importance to him. "I'll wait for you," she whispered.

She walked out of the house with him and he kissed her, his mouth tracing the familiar curve of hers, his arms holding her very close. Then he was gone, hurrying to his snowmobile and waving to her as he disappeared in the direction of Raedar. She watched him go until he was an indistinct dot against the white dusk, but he did not look around or wave again.

Tony Kobuk rode Bethany back when he returned from school and stayed to frolic with the dogs. She was glad of the company, sorry when the teen-ager left. The cabin had never felt so lonely, so isolated, and the winds that night were harsh, the forerunner of a storm system that was threatening to burst through the long spell of clear, dry weather. She missed Griff terribly, heard him half a dozen times in the noises made by the cabin or the wind. She wished that he would come soon. What kind of business was keeping him so long away from her?

She cooked enough supper for two, but Griff did not arrive in time for the meal. Nor had he come when she put the dogs into the indoor kennel against the possibility of the storm's hitting that night. Later, she lay in bed trying for sleep and missing him. Her wakefulness bothered her. How many nights would she lie awake waiting for Griff after they were married? Maria Bluett had said that one could get used to anything, but she wondered if she could ever adjust to the lonely waiting. She had never minded being alone before, had enjoyed silence and solitude and quiet independence. Now she felt only half alive without Griff.

Toward midnight she fell asleep and awakened in the morning to find herself still alone. The storm had not quite broken yet, but the air was heavy with wind and impending snow as she hurried through her chores. What could be keeping Griff? she wondered. There was one way of finding out. Perhaps his busi-

ness was still continuing, would imprison him in
Raedar for a good part of the day. If that were so, she
wanted to be with him.

She harnessed the dogs and as she drove her team
toward Tilikit, she thought of Griff. Last night's loneliness had proved something to her. Living without
Griff was not really living. Perhaps what Julie had
said was true—she must be willing to compromise on
many thing she had not been willing to compromise on
before. As she pulled her team into Tilikit, she found
herself wanting the feel of Griff's arms around her,
his lips on hers.

Her heart leaped when she saw his snowmobile
before the Kobuks' house. She barely waited to hitch
her team securely before running inside and was
greeted by Julie's surprised exclamation.

"You have ESP or something, Bethy? I was just
going to send Tony to find you."

For a moment fear squeezed her heart. Could the
accident Griff had had with the moose have brought
complications? But Julie was explaining. "Griff just
got back from Raedar. He's been there all night,
Bethy. He just came back to pack a few things. The
plane's coming to take him to Raedar in an hour."

What plane? But before she could question, Griff
came into the room. He showed no sign of having
worked all night, and his voice was crisp as he
started to ask Julie a question. Then, seeing Bethany,
the words died away. For a second, she saw that odd,
shadowed look veil his green gaze.

"Beth!" he exclaimed. "How did you get here so
quickly?"

He came forward to take her into his arms, bulky as
she was in her parka. He kissed her, lips warm
against her cheek. She breathed deep of him for a
moment and then stepped away. "Julie says you're
leaving?" she asked. He nodded.

"It came up very suddenly, Beth. Hal Bluett's radio message was to tell me that negotiations with Halstead have taken a sudden and critical turn. They need me in New York right away."

"I'll make sure your bags are packed," Julie said tactfully, as she left the room. Bethany heard her departure but her eyes were steady on Griff. This would happen, she thought, and happen again. Wherever they lived, Griff would be called away—and she would have to get used to it.

"I'll miss you," she said softly.

He sighed and gathered her close again, and for a moment the tension and air of business about him dissolved. "I'm going to miss you like hell." He paused and then added, "Come with me, Beth! Tony will care for your dogs again. You can buy any things you need in New York. This time we'll do the town as it should be done."

She shook her head regretfully. "I can't. The Rohn's too close, and I have to keep both our teams in top shape. Tony can help me run the dogs." She paused. "Just hurry back to me."

To her surprise he dropped his arms around her and stepped away.

"That mightn't be possible, Beth," he said.

"What do you mean?" There was something wrong, something more than a projected business trip in the wind. She followed him as he turned his back on her and walked toward the big wood stove in the Kobuks' living area and stood with his hands splayed over its warmth. "What is it, Griff?"

"There's no easy way, so I'll say it right out. I'm needed in New York for the duration. I have to be there from now until Halstead really becomes a part of Deane Enterprises." He hesitated and then said, "It could take weeks."

Bewildered, she searched his averted face. "But

the Rohn comes up in a couple of weeks—it's coming right around Christmas time. Remember?"

"I didn't anticipate this new development. Even if something like this came up, I was sure it wouldn't happen until after the Rohn." He turned to her now, the unhappiness obvious in his eyes and line of mouth. "I'm damnably sorry, Beth. I can't be your partner in the relay. That's out."

Chapter Fourteen

❧

Could she believe what he was saying? She could not. She stared at him. How could he stand there and tell her such things? "You don't mean it!" she exclaimed.

His mouth was suddenly a grim line. "I do, unfortunately. It's not just my decision. Deane Enterprises is a huge corporation, and a deal like this involves not just millions of dollars but people as well. My personal feelings just don't count."

But they did—she knew they did. It was Griff's philosophy through and through. First the power and the money, and then the "personal feelings." And what about her feelings and his commitment to her? "So we scrap everything just like that?" she forced herself to ask.

Guilt, unhappiness, and impatience warred in his eyes. "Look, I feel wretched about it. I'll do whatever you like. You told me it wasn't too late to get another partner, didn't you? Why not contact one right away? I'll make it worth his while to run my team, partner you."

He was up to his old tricks, using money to make everything right. Though he recognized her disappointment, he brushed it aside as unimportant against the great goals of his corporate takeover. Anger filled her, so mixed with hurt that she seemed heavy with pain. While she had been missing him terribly, while she, in her secret heart, had decided to sacrifice her world and make his life-style hers, he had not been thinking of her at all. Love had not made one jot of difference in the separateness of their minds.

"I'll make sure you don't lose out in this," he was saying. His voice was more confident now. "I know that you've spent a lot of time and money training for the event. I know what it means to you. You'll get your trophy, Beth."

He was offering her the trophy as if that solved everything. "Do you think you can buy me off like that?" She whispered.

He frowned. "For God's sake, Beth. It's just one race."

Carefully, she controlled the tremor in her voice to answer him. "Was it 'just' a race when you left your precious corporation and came to Tilikit to find me? For weeks you acted as if winning the Rohn was a big thing in your life. You made me think it mattered. That I mattered. Now, without discussing it with me, you want to throw it all away. How like you, Griff!"

He made an impatient sound. "Look, we can discuss this later. My plane will be here soon and I want to beat the storm out of Raedar."

"Don't worry. You'll meet your plane on time. And if not, it will wait for you. Everything revolves around you, doesn't it?" How could her voice sound so firm when the rest of her was breaking up within her like shattered ice in a frozen sea? "You call the tune and everybody dances to it. You choose, nobody else. And you love challenge. Was that why you came after me so hard? Because I wouldn't give in to you right away?" The angry impatience in his eyes hurt worse than anything she had ever encountered, and she turned away. "I trusted you," she whispered.

He did not hear her last, murmured words. He was

tired and unhappy about the decisions he had had to make, and now she was infuriating him with her inability to understand. "See sense," he argued. "Look, I know you're upset now, but we'll talk again later. I'll contact you on the radio as soon as I get to New York."

"No," she said, "we won't ever talk again."

This had to be finished now, finished forever. She couldn't bleed for him time and time again, couldn't play his games and wait until he chose the time to love her. He had talked of making choices, and now she was making one. "Good-bye, Griff," she said steadily.

He crossed the room in swift strides and caught her shoulders, whirling her to face him. He looked shaken, unhappy, angry. But Griff Deane the great mogul, the loved and respected and revered, would not like his conquests showing *him* the door!

"Beth, don't be a fool. You know what you mean to me," he said. For a treacherous moment her heart wavered, and then he said, "All this fuss for one damned relay race. How much is the prize? I'll give you the money right now, if you like."

Carefully she raised her hands and pried his away from her shoulders. Then, she turned blindly and walked out of the Kobuks' front door. At the door she paused but did not turn to face him. "I don't want your money or any part of you," she said. "I never want to see you again, Griff."

And outside, unhitching her dogs and getting into her sled she thought, You'll see. I'll get another partner and we'll win. And when the prize money comes I'll send you my share. Damn you, Griff Deane.

She thought she heard the house door open and half turned, the face of the house shifting in the blur of her tears. He had not come. He would never come to her again. Tears caught in her long eyelashes as she called to her dogs. This would be the very last time that she would cry for Griff, she swore to herself. From now until forever she would only trust and rely on herself.

That day she took her dogs out onto the trails and worked them and herself until exhaustion caked her face with sweat and the stinging snow of the newly risen storm. She was grateful to see the silhouette of her cabin, but her relief was swirled time out of mind, hurled away in the sudden leap of all her pulses as she saw that a snowmobile stood before the cabin door. Lights winked in the cabin window, Griff, her heart shouted exultantly.

She called the dogs to halt and jumped from the sled, racing the last yards between her and the cabin. But as she neared the snowmobile, her heart sank. This was not Griff's superb new machine but an old and beat up model—Julie Kobuk's. Disappointment turned to dread as she realized that Julie had probably come out here to talk about Griff. If he's sent her, if she says anything to try and change my mind, I won't listen, she thought, and her soft mouth set stubbornly.

Inside the cabin, however, there was a surprise. Julie hadn't come alone. With her was a short, muscular young Eskimo man, a driver Bethany recognized even before Julie waved a big hand in his direction.

"You two know each other? Bethany Sheridan, Ben Mihailouk. He's been looking for a partner for the Rohn."

"I had a partner, but he broke his leg in three places last week—a freak accident." Ben's voice was calm and pleasant, and his face was pleasant also: black-browned, black-eyed, relaxed. "It was really tough luck since we both put a lot into training for the race. Now I'm hoping that maybe I can recoup something and split it with him." He paused. "I've heard you're kind of in the same boat I am."

"Sort of." Bethany glanced at Julie, and her friend's eyes met hers frankly. A surge of gratitude rose in her as she realized Julie hadn't come from Griff at all but to help her meet her unhappiness and conquer it. For the first time since this morning, she felt her spirits lift. "I'd like to talk about it some more, Ben, if you have time."

Ben had time. Julie had time. In the honored tradition of the wilderness they sat and had tea, talked of dogs and hunting, of the new schoolhouse in Raedar which would be constructed in time for Ben's little daughter, Katrina, to attend. Finally, they spoke of racing.

"I know you're one fine racer, Bethany," Ben said. "I'd be proud to be your partner for the Rohn. If you'd like to maybe try things out for a week or so, see how we go together . . ."

"No!" She hadn't realized how vehemently she spoke until she saw the surprise in his eyes. She tried to amend her tone with a smile. "The Rohn is too close by. I'd say we should start right in training, Ben. I want to win it as much as you do."

"Go for it." Julie said softly. Her black eyes were proud and affectionate. "Go for it, Bethy. Like I said, you're racing with a winner now, Ben."

A winner—partnered with a winner. She shut her eyes to close out the image of a far different face, dark, aquiline, the face of a conqueror, a maurauder. Go away, Griff, she thought, while memory tied itself into a tight, hurtful knot inside her heart. I do not want to remember you. I will not think of you again.

In the days that followed, she grimly kept her bargain with herself. She worked hard with Ben, worked hard alone at her chores or with her dogs. She would not compromise, would not allow any weakening of her guard. When Ben understandably asked about the rift between herself and Griff, she simply said that it was a matter of business on his part. "He had more important things to do," she said, and Ben's dark eyes flashed understanding.

"These *cheechako* types are all alike, really," he told her. "They don't look at things the way we do, Bethy."

Ben was a tireless and conscientious partner, an excellent driver, and soon they were working well together on their runs. She was glad at their cooperation, pleased that they very definitely had a chance to win the relay. But the relay no longer filled her mind with pleasure as it had used to, and her desire for the trophy had ebbed into something very much like indifference. That sense of uncaring seemed to flow into other areas of her life as well, and as she sat in her cabin, she was filled with restlessness and an emotion she refused to recognize as loneliness.

Sometimes the feelings got so bad that she would bring Katiktok into the cabin to stay with her, laughing at the dog's expression as it begged for scraps or stretched blissfully on its back by the fire. But this was not the companionship she needed, no matter how she denied it. In her dreams, Talka searched not for Nonak but for Griff, and she moaned his name like the questing wind. No matter how hard she tried, she could not help those dreams. Often she woke with arms outstretched, reaching for him.

Griff had been in contact with the Kobuks since his departure, but Bethany wouldn't let Julie talk about it. The one time she tried, she shook her head, stopping the older woman.

"It's finished, Julie. Water under the ice. Forget it—I've forgotten."

"Have you?" Julie asked. She hesitated, then shook her head in preamble to saying something controversial. "Elmer says to mind my own business, but I care too much about you. That Griff did wrong by leaving you high and dry, but I told you about men one time, Bethy. They need their corporations, their toys. Griff made the wrong decision this time, that's all. He still loves you."

She laughed on a hard note that stood against a wall of tears.

"Like fun he does!"

Julie shook her head again. "Your voice is telling me you care. Huh! You've dropped weight and you look about as good as an old crow in winter." She paused. "And your heart's not in this race anymore. Is it?"

Bethany was startled. "Did Ben say so?"

"He doesn't know you like I do," Julie pointed out. "You probably will win, because you're a good sportswoman, Bethy. Only Elmer and me and people who love you are going to know you're losing something in your heart even while you're winning the trophy."

After her talk with Julie, Bethany was careful. Around the Kobuks she took care to laugh, talk more. When Julie invited her to help trim the Christmas tree at their home, she went and was full of Christmas carols and ate two helpings of the good food Julie served. And when the talk strayed to the upcoming Rohn, she took great care to sound interested.

Elmer said that though the Rohn was a week away, dogsled racers from all over the country were already flocking into Settlers Bay.

"It's going to be one big mess down there with the drivers and the dogs and their gear, not to mention the tourists and the gawkers," Elmer commented. "You glad it's coming at last, Bethy?"

She nodded. She was glad, but not in the way Elmer thought. The Rohn would always be tied in some way to Griff, to the memory of all they had shared and could not share. What I really need is to put the Rohn behind me and then go on, she thought. The Iditarod, maybe?

And, as if she had flicked a mental button, she remembered the laughter in his green eyes, the quirk of his lips. "It'll be my pleasure to beat you in the Iditarod, Bethany." Her fingers almost went numb, and she nearly dropped the plate she was holding. Would everything and everyone remind her of Griff from this day forward?

Driving home she told herself that she would need to monitor herself more carefully. I got over Piers, she thought, and I'll get over Griff, too. She said it to herself, a litany she only half believed, as she fed her dogs and sat alone in the sauna, trying to relax in the warm steam. She said it to herself as she tossed between the sheets of the suddenly too-big bed and as she did so she found herself wondering where Griff lay tonight, and whether he was alone.

No, she thought. He can't be. He'll be with someone new—someone he doesn't have to love or need. Someone who doesn't trust him and cares about the things he wants—money and power. She tried to hold onto this picture of Griff but it wavered and, despite her efforts, collapsed around her as she remembered him as he had been. Loving, warm, full of laughter, passionate with a primal desire that matched her own. My Beth, my Beth—his words seemed to hang on the still air about her, and suddenly loneliness was too hard to bear, too great even for tears.

"I'll never forget him," she whispered out loud

into the darkness, and as she did so saw the ripple and play of the great northern lights that shone through her window and onto her bed. Like the glorious lights, Griff's and her love had been brief and soon over. And yet, while it had lasted, she had felt, given, received more than she had from any man, would ever again. "God help me, I still love him," she said, and having admitted this lay still and watched the rings of a faraway light move and glide over her lonely bed.

Next day she noticed that Ben Mihailouk was oddly silent. His usual cheerfulness was blunted, and he appeared thoughtful, almost preoccupied as they drove the dogs in last-minute maneuvers and patterns across the snow. Finally, she asked him point blank what was wrong.

He hesitated and then looked her straight in the eye. "I was wondering about the partnership for the Rohn," he said. She stared at him and he said, with embarrassment, "I was wondering if you were trying to find a way to back out of the deal. You know I'd understand completely if you wanted to have things the way they were before I came on the scene."

"I haven't got the slightest idea what you're talking about," she said, and her blood went suddenly cold and icy as he told her.

"I thought that you and Griff Deane would want to pick up your partnership. You two trained a lot longer than we did, I know, and it was just business that messed that up. Now he's back in Raedar, I just figured you'd want to go back to the original plan."

Griff here—back in the north? But the Kobuks hadn't seemed to have known last night, and she certainly hadn't had an inkling. For what had he come if not the Rohn? But if that were so, why hadn't he contacted her?

"How did you find out?" she heard herself ask quite calmly, and Ben said that he'd seen the Aztec land in the landing field in Raedar. Griff had been on the plane, of this he was sure.

"No mistaking that dude," he said, grinning, then sobered. "If you were worried about our arrangement, don't let it bother you, Bethany. I know a commitment is a commitment."

But not to Griff—never to Griff. Carefully she took a breath, afraid that she might burst into tears or shatter if she did. She did neither, and she even managed a smile. "Don't be silly, Ben. I think it's a pretty bad way of getting rid of me, and it's not going to work." He looked surprised but pleased as she added, "Remember? You're going to win that prize money for you and your first partner."

But as they resumed their racing, she could hardly see. She drove on instinct alone, all her other senses at work in trying to puzzle out what was happening. Why had Griff come? He certainly could not be seeking out a new partner. Perhaps he had come merely to dispose of sled and dogs, close this part of his life. But if that were the reason, why wouldn't he simply have contacted the Kobuks and asked them to take care of things for him?

She had no answers to this question then or later, when Ben left her off at the cabin and drove his own team back to Raedar. She had half hoped that she would find Griff's snowmobile by her door, but of course it was not there. In the morning, she thought, I'll go into Tilikit and ask Julie. Or will I? She hesitated over that problem, at last decided to do nothing. Perhaps Ben had been mistaken. Even if he were right, obviously Griff had not come to see her.

Even so, she slept worse than she usually did that night. When at last she fell asleep at dawn it was a drugged, fitful sleep that found her tired and restless in the morning. She wanted nothing more than to turn around and go back to sleep, but dogs needed to be fed and run, chores must be done. Sighing, she dressed, and hefting the heavy metal pails she went down the familiar pathway to the lake.

It was very cold today. Christmas coming soon, she thought, trying to cheer herself with that thought. She would spend the time with Julie and her family—and hopefully, she'd have a trophy to present to the Kobuks as a Christmas gift. She wanted no part of keeping this trophy. She . . .

Her thoughts died away as she suddenly saw the large dark shape in her way. Moose or caribou? Both were possible. She had seen both large animals come this way this late in the winter. She would stand very still and let the big beast move on.

But the solid dark shape did not move. Her heart began to thump with painful apprehension that evolved into a more painful certainty. No, she thought, no.

Then, the shadow spoke. "Beth," it said.

It was, of course, Griff.

Chapter Fifteen

❦

For long moments she simply stood there, unable to move or speak. He had come, after all. For what? What did he want from her?

"Aren't you even going to say hello?" Griff was asking. His voice in the dark coldness was decidedly cheery, much too cheerful after their last parting and the long silence in between. Moreover, he sounded relaxed. Whatever he'd come for, he certainly wasn't anticipating a return to the argument they had had before he left on corporate business.

She molded her own voice into coolness. "What are you doing here? I thought your business was going to keep you tied up until after the Rohn."

"So did I—but things speeded up a lot." A pause. "I hear that things are going well for you. I knew you'd get a good partner, and this Ben Mihailouk seems excellent. I've heard some good things about him."

He was up to his old tricks. She was assailed by contradictory feelings. Part of her was furious that he could just blithely show up like this with no reference to what had happened on their last meeting. The other, treacherous part of her ached to rush across the dark separating them and hurl herself into his arms.

"You heard right, then," she said. "Ben and I are going to win the relay together."

He started to walk toward her and she tensed so sharply that the water slopped out of her buckets. He merely took the buckets from her. "Don't be silly," he said, when she protested this action. "You've already spilled more than half of your daily supply. I'll walk you back to the cabin and you can offer me some true wilderness hospitality. I could use some hot coffee while we talk."

Irritation spurted as she said, "You have a short memory. When we dissolved our partnership before you left for New York, we decided not to see each other again."

"You decided," he pointed out. His voice seemed suddenly rougher as they came within the circle of the cabin's light. "I've missed you," he said.

She would not listen. She would never let him move her again. She turned to face him and saw that the glow from the window had framed his face in gold. For a moment her loneliness for him, all the starvations her senses had endured in his absence, reached out to him. Then, she had hold of herself. Never again, she thought.

"I meant what I said, Griff. We no longer have anything to discuss."

He set the buckets down onto the ground with such force that more water slopped out. "If you'd just listen to me—"

"What could you possibly say to me? I won't listen!" she cried. "Are you going to offer me money to come back to you? You can't expect to just walk out of your commitments and my life and then stroll back into it."

For a moment the green in his eyes blazed emerald. Then, the light died as suddenly as it had come. "Of course you're right," he said. He sounded regretful but not unhappy. "At least it gives me the chance to apologize for what happened that day. I regretted the necessity of breaking my commitment to you, but as I explained, it was unavoidable."

The consummate businessman, the corporate giant! He did not care about her, could not. If he had, he would not be talking about regret and apology and necessity. What would he have done if she had followed her foolish instincts and thrown herself into his arms?

"What brings you back to Alaska?" she asked carefully, and was proud of her even tone.

"Business," he responded promptly. "Deane Enterprises is considering the possibility of a branch office in Anchorage, and while I was in Raedar for the Rohn I spoke to some very good local people— people who might want to come aboard and work for that branch office." He paused. "Besides, I did want to thank the Kobuks personally for all they'd done for me."

He sounded so calm and reasonable that she knew he was telling nothing but the unvarnished truth. He had not come to see her at all. When she had severed their partnership, it had died. As for his love for her—had he ever loved her? Had he returned already to the creed his father had once taught him: that to need someone was the pathway to hell?

"Well, then," she said, "now that you've come and done what you planned to do, I suppose you'll be leaving."

He nodded. "I won't be around for the Rohn. I'm spending Christmas with Hal and Maria; I'll be returning to New York as soon as possible." He hesitated, then added, "The Bluetts send their love and best wishes. Good luck, Bethany. I know you'll win the relay—you were always a winner."

That was a lie. She was losing him now. He was walking away from her, and against all pride or reason her lips formed his name. She moved forward, hands outstretched to him, but he did not turn around and see her, nor did he hear her. Without a backward glance he walked to his snowmobile. Then, he waved.

She stood still where he had left her long after he had gone, and she felt the gold of her cabin's light dim into grayness around her. The world would always be in half-light from now on, she thought dismally. There could be no color, no substance now that he was gone. And yet, what else had there been to do? What could have happened save this? He had said not one word of love or regret. He did not want her anymore, and there was no altering or denying reality. She had done the only thing she could.

Wearily, she picked up her pails of water and then realized that what Griff had said was true. The pails were only half full, and she would need more water by the end of the day. I'll need to go back for more, she thought numbly, and pouring water from one bucket to the other, she started back down the pathway to the lake.

She could hardly feel her feet as she walked. She did not even realize that she was crying as she went. Only when she stooped to fill her bucket did she pause to wipe her streaming eyes, and as if this action were a catalyst, she began to sob. She could not control her sobbing and her sense of desolation, and here where no one could see her, she wept aloud. She had once sworn that she would never again cry for him, and in a sense she was not breaking that promise. Now she was crying for herself, for the long years that stretched before her in void and emptiness, for the loss of her heart and her soul. How long she stood there she had no idea, but finally she pulled herself together, wiped the rapidly freezing tears from her cheeks, and again tried to fill her bucket.

It wasn't easy. She couldn't see the hole in the ice because of her tears, and the water kept spilling. "Damn!" she finally exclaimed in exasperation.

"You're not doing it right."

He could not be standing near her—but he was. She almost cried out loud as he took the bucket from her and filled it with that easy, scooping motion she remembered. He set it down on the ice and then turned to her.

"Beth—" he began, and then stopped. She could see him frown in the dusky dawn. "Why are you crying?" he demanded.

She had no defenses left this time. Tears had stripped her of her last shreds of dignity, and she could no longer keep the wall between them. "You," she whispered.

"Oh, Beth," he said, and gathered her into his arms, held her so tight that she could not breathe. "Say it again," he said, his voice muffled. "Tell me you're crying because you didn't want to see me go."

"You know why I'm crying. You know! And I swore never to cry for you again . . ." he stopped her words by tilting back her head and kissing her, his lips warm and knowledgeable, his lean face dazed with joy.

"I swear you never will again. Beth, my love—"

She clung to him. Wrong or right, mad or sane— did it matter? He was her world and she was with him. What had been halved was whole again. A warmth that had been so lately frozen began to run through her, filling her with light as he spoke quickly, the words tumbling out of him unlike his usual decisive speech.

"I said I loved you, and I did. But I didn't know much about really loving, Beth. I still had this idea that love was something convenient. You would fit into my world, somehow. You would learn to compromise. When this thing with Halstead came up, I regretted the Rohn but I felt sure that you really would understand. When you didn't, I thought it was your fault. This was what happened, I told myself, when I *needed* another human being. I was furious at you when you walked out on me. I swore that I'd never come to you, never think of you again."

"But . . . but you said you came here on business," she whispered.

He laughed a rueful, self-mocking little laugh. "I can lie to myself very nicely. I left Hal negotiating the last phases of the Halstead deal and flew to Anchorage because I assured myself and my people that there was a great potential market for Deane goods in the north. I never admitted to myself that I wanted to be closer to you, that I wanted to see you, that you were more important to me than anything else in the world."

She could not quite believe what he was saying, could not quite adjust to the warmth of his arms. It was too sudden, this shift from sorrow to joy. She said slowly, "You actually left someone else in charge of your precious Halstead deal?"

He nodded. "It didn't seem that all-consuming anymore. I missed you as soon as I left Raedar, you know. I saw you in everything, everyone I met." Quietly, carefully, as if his words were the bridge over a great gulf of emptiness he added, "It has been so lonely without you, my love."

She saw it finally, irrevocably in his eyes. She saw the tenderness there, the need of her that had brought him all these miles against his training and his doubts and his pride. "I missed you terribly," she whispered. "I thought that without you I might die of loneliness. But I didn't die, Griff. The days just kept on getting longer and more empty and so gray and lifeless."

He bent his dark head and kissed her, his lips sweet, relearning the welcome perimeters of her mouth. My love, he thought, my dear love; and relief and triumph sang through him as he held her closer. "When I saw you a little while ago, I wanted to sweep you into my arms like this. But when you were so cold I knew I'd forfeited all claim to your love. So I drove away without saying a word, and I'd have kept on going, too, except that I came to that spot where my snowmobile broke down in the storm. Remember?" she nodded, and he said tenderly, "I remembered how I felt when I saw your face through the whirl of snow. And I knew that if I let you go out of my life there'd be no happiness or hope for me."

She whispered his name and drew his face down to meet her lips again, but he stopped her almost sternly. "We've got to discuss something," he told her. "I want to say this now, say it to you once and for always. I will never lose you again. I cannot bear the thought. If you marry me, I agree to live wherever you wish. Wilderness or city or anywhere in between—I will go where you want to go."

Whither thou goest, I will go. Her heart was swelling with such happiness that his image misted in sudden tears. "Oh, Griff, it doesn't matter *where* anymore," she told him. She gave a little laugh that crested on a sob. "While you were gone—even before that—my cabin was lonely without you. I knew then that I could raise my dogs anywhere, race or not race, just as long as we were together." She hesitated. "There's just one problem: the Rohn. It matters to Ben, and he's counting on me to help him win it. I can't just walk out on him. Will you understand if I can't come to the city and spend Christmas with you and the Bluetts?"

His smile was sweet beyond imagining. "I've decided that there's nothing I'd like more than a genuine Eskimo Christmas," he said. "Hal and Maria will understand. And beyond the thrill of watching my new wife win the Rohn, there's something to be said for Arctic honeymoons."

She nestled back into his arms, too full of love for him to speak. She felt as she had felt long ago, that there would never be enough time to show him all her love or ways enough to express the closeness she felt for him. As if he read her thought, he began to kiss her with small, somehow intimate kisses.

"Perhaps it's time we got back to the cabin?" he suggested softly.

She nodded happy agreement. "High time." She smiled against the sweet, remembered promise of his lips.

Don't go to bed without Romance!

- Contemporaries
- Romances
- Historicals
- Suspense

- Forthcoming Titles
- Author Profiles
- Book Reviews
- How-To-Write Tips

Read

Romantic Times

your guide to the next
two months' best books.
44 page bi-monthly tabloid • 6 Issues $8.95

Send your order to: New American Library, P.O. Box 999, Bergenfield, NJ 07621.
Make check or money order payable to: New American Library
I enclose $_____ in ☐ check ☐ money order (no CODs or cash)   **RT**
or charge ☐ MasterCard ☐ Visa

CARD #_____ EXP. DATE_____

SIGNATURE_____

NAME_____

ADDRESS_____

CITY_____STATE____ZIP_____

Please allow at least 8 weeks for delivery. Offer subject to change or withdrawal without notice

RAPTURE ROMANCE—*Reader's Opinion Questionnaire*

Thank you for filling out our questionnaire. Your response to the following questions will help us to bring you more and better books, by telling us what you are like, what you look for in a romance, and how we can best keep you informed about our books. Your opinions are important to us, and we appreciate your help.

1. What made you choose this particular book? (This book is #_____)
   Art on the front cover_____
   Plot descriptions on the back cover_____
   Friend's recommendation_____
   Other (please specify)_____

2. Would you rate this book:
   Excellent_____   Very good_____   Good_____
   Fair_____   Poor_____

3. What did you like most about the book?
   Heroine_____ Hero_____ Setting_____ Plot_____
   Other (please specify)_____

4. Were the love scenes (circle answer):
   Too explicit   Not explicit enough   Just right

5. Are Rapture Romances:
   Too long_____   Too short_____   Just right_____

6. How many Rapture Romances have you read?_____

7. Number, from most favorite to least favorite, romance lines you enjoy:
   Avon Finding Mr. Right_____
   Ballantine Love and Life_____
   Bantam Loveswept_____
   Dell Candlelight Ecstasy_____
   Jove Second Chance at Love_____
   Harlequin_____
   Harlequin Presents_____
   Harlequin Super Romance_____
   Rapture Romance_____
   Silhouette_____
   Silhouette Intimate Moments_____
   Silhouette Desire_____
   Silhouette Special Edition_____

8. Please check the types of romances you enjoy:
   Historical romance_____
   Regency romance_____
   Romantic suspense_____
   Short, light contemporary romance_____
   Short, sensual contemporary romance_____
   Longer contemporary romance_____

9. What is the age of the oldest _____ youngest _____ heroine you would like to read about? The oldest _____ youngest _____ hero?

10. What elements do you dislike in a romance?
    Mystery/suspense_____ Supernatural_____
    Other (please specify)_____

11. We would like to know:
    ● How much television you watch
      Over 4 hours a day_____ 2–4 hours a day_____
      0–2 hours a day_____
    ● What your favorite programs are
      _____
      _____
    ● When you usually watch television
      8 a.m. to 5 p.m._____ 5 p.m. to 11 p.m._____
      11 p.m. to 2 a.m._____

12. How many magazines do you read regularly?
    More than 6_____ 3–6_____ 0–3_____
    Which of these are your favorites?
    _____
    _____

To get a picture of our readers, and to know where to reach them, the following personal information will be most helpful, if you don't mind giving it, and will be kept only for our records.

Name_____
Address_____
City_____
State_____Zip code_____

Please check your age group:
  17 and under_____
  18–34_____
  35–49_____
  50–64_____
  65 and older_____

Education:
  Now in high school_____
  Now in college_____
  Graduated from high school_____
  Completed some college_____
  Graduated from college_____

Are you now working outside the home?
  Yes_____ No_____
  Full time_____
  Part time_____
  Job title_____

Thank you for your time and effort. Please send the complete questionnaire and answer sheet to: Robin Grunder, RAPTURE ROMANCE, New American Library, 1633 Broadway, New York, NY 10019

RAPTURE ROMANCE

**Provocative and sensual,
passionate and tender—
the magic and mystery of love
in all its many guises**

COMING NEXT MONTH

ROMANTIC CAPER by Melinda McKenzie. They were an unlikely pair for romance: Diana Bach, daughter of an infamous jewel thief, and Ivre Smyth-George, Scotland Yard inspector. And though love sparkled between them, Ivre didn't quite trust Diana. How could she convince him that the only thing she wanted to steal was his heart. . . ?

SILVER DAWN by Valerie Zayne. Against her will, Lia Cooper was drawn to mercurial entrepreneur Brett Rayner's magnetic vitality. But once he had stormed her defenses and unlocked her passions, would he move on to a new challenge . . . and a new love?

ORCHID OF LOVE by Kathryn Kent. Jackie Allison was determined to be a success in business. And with the help of dynamic Cal Prescott, her dream was coming true. But Cal taught her far more than just business, claiming her heart and awakening her body to an all-consuming passion. Jackie couldn't picture life without Cal, but she didn't know if he felt the same way. . . .

CHANSON D'AMOUR by Ann McClure. Mara Sullivan melted under Luc de Montbard's burning gaze and she gave herself to him in a moment of wild desire. But the successful real estate agent had come to France to convince Luc to sell his property. Mara wondered how she could prove her love was real—and not a crazy scheme to get his land . . .

"THE ROMANCE WRITER'S MANUAL . . . A VERITA-
BLE ENCYCLOPEDIA OF ROMANCE GOODIES."
—*Chicago Sun-Times*

HOW TO WRITE A ROMANCE AND GET IT PUBLISHED

by Kathryn Falk,
editor of *Romantic Times*

Intimate advice from the world's top romance writers:

JENNIFER WILDE · BARBARA CARTLAND · JANET DAILEY · PATRICIA MATTHEWS · JUDE DEVERAUX · BERTRICE SMALL · JAYNE CASTLE · ROBERTA GELLIS · PATRICIA GALLAGHER · CYNTHIA WRIGHT

No one understands how to write a successful, saleable romance better than Kathryn Falk. Now she has written the best, most comprehensive guide to writing and publishing romance fiction ever— for both beginners and professional writers alike. From the field's top writers, agents, and editors come tips on:

- FINDING THE FORMULA: ROMANCE RULES
- SELECTING A GENRE: FROM HISTORICALS TO TEEN ROMANCE
- LISTINGS OF PUBLISHING HOUSES, EDITORS, AGENTS
- WRITING SERIES AND SAGAS
- THE AUTHOR-AGENT RELATIONSHIP
- ADVICE FOR MEN, HUSBANDS, AND WRITING TEAMS

"The definitive aspiring romance writer's self-help book . . . lively, interesting, thorough." —*New York Daily News*

(0451—129032—$4.95)

Buy them at your local bookstore or use this convenient coupon for ordering.

NEW AMERICAN LIBRARY
P.O. Box 999, Bergenfield, New Jersey 07621
Please send me the books I have checked above. I am enclosing $_____
(please add $1.00 to this order to cover postage and handling). Send check
or money order—no cash or C.O.D.'s. Prices and numbers are subject to change
without notice.

Name_____

Address_____

City _____ State _____ Zip Code _____

Allow 4-6 weeks for delivery.
This offer is subject to withdrawal without notice.

RAPTURE ROMANCE

**Provocative and sensual,
passionate and tender—
the magic and mystery of love
in all its many guises**

New Titles Available Now

(0451)

#73 ☐ **AFFAIR OF THE HEART by Joan Wolf.** Caroline Carruthers was lost when Jay Hamilton took her in his arms and swept her into a tantalizing affair. But the ambassador's daughter and the handsome rancher were so unalike. Would the passion that drew them together be enough to withstand their differences. . . ? (129113—$1.95)*

#74 ☐ **PURELY PHYSICAL by Kasey Adams.** Diet and exercise helped Rachel Scott become the sleek, sensuous woman her old friend David Gearhart wanted as a lover. And though she had always loved David and would no matter how he looked, Rachel didn't know if she could say the same about his feelings. . . . (129121—$1.95)*

#75 ☐ **LOVER'S RUN by Francine Shore.** Arrogant business tycoon Griff Deane left Bethany Sheridan feeling cold—until his bold kisses melted her icy reserve and left her burning with desire. But Bethany had to know if his love was real, or if he was only using her for his own selfish reasons. . . . (129628—$2.95)

#76 ☐ **RIPTIDE by Deborah Benét.** Artist Whitney Campbell found Detective Anthony Tallwalker's charm irresistible, and soon the two were caught in a whirlpool of passion. But as Whitney lost her heart, she wondered if she could live with a man whose life was always on the line. . . . (129636—$1.95)*

*Price is $2.25 in Canada

To order, use coupon on the last page.

RAPTURE ROMANCE

Provocative and sensual,
passionate and tender—
the magic and mystery of love
in all its many guises

Buy them at your local

bookstore or use coupon

on next page for ordering.

RAPTURE ROMANCE

Provocative and sensual, passionate and tender— the magic and mystery of love in all its many guises

(0451)

#45	☐	SEPTEMBER SONG by Lisa Moore.	(126301—$1.95)*
#46	☐	A MOUNTAIN MAN by Megan Ashe.	(126319—$1.95)*
#47	☐	THE KNAVE OF HEARTS by Estelle Edwards.	(126327—$1.95)*
#48	☐	BEYOND ALL STARS by Linda McKenzie.	(126335—$1.95)*
#49	☐	DREAMLOVER by JoAnn Robb.	(126343—$1.95)*
#50	☐	A LOVE SO FRESH by Marilyn Davids.	(126351—$1.95)*
#51	☐	LOVER IN THE WINGS by Francine Shore.	(127617—$1.95)*
#52	☐	SILK AND STEEL by Kathryn Kent.	(127625—$1.95)*
#53	☐	ELUSIVE PARADISE by Eleanor Frost.	(127633—$1.95)*
#54	☐	RED SKY AT NIGHT by Ellie Winslow.	(127641—$1.95)*
#55	☐	BITTERSWEET TEMPTATION by Jillian Roth.	(127668—$1.95)*
#56	☐	SUN SPARK by Nina Coombs.	(127676—$1.95)*

*Price is $2.25 in Canada.

Buy them at your local bookstore or use this convenient coupon for ordering.
NEW AMERICAN LIBRARY
P.O. Box 999, Bergenfield, New Jersey 07621
Please send me the books I have checked above. I am enclosing $_____
(please add $1.00 to this order to cover postage and handling). Send check
or money order—no cash or C.O.D.'s. Prices and numbers are subject to change
without notice.

Name_____

Address_____

City _____ State _____ Zip Code _____
Allow 4-6 weeks for delivery.
This offer is subject to withdrawal without notice.

RAPTURE ROMANCE

Provocative and sensual, passionate and tender— the magic and mystery of love in all its many guises

---

Buy them at your local bookstore or use coupon on next page for ordering.

ON SALE NOW!

Signet's daring new historical romance ...

A firestorm of romance and passion sears a young American beauty's heart in the splendour of imperial Russia

JOURNEY TO DESIRE
by Helene Thornton

Laura Holman, a beautiful American flower, had no defenses agianst the experienced kisses of the dashing young nobleman, Penn Allandale. He ignited in her a woman's deepest longings, but too soon she was forced to leave his caresses behind when she traveled to Tsarist Russia with her artist father. It was there, amidst the magnificent palaces and lavish riches that she met a darkly handsome Romanov prince who schemed to conquer her body and soul. But for Laurel a journey to desire could have but one destination—and she followed her tender heart along a perilous path, searching for the one man who would offer her love's shimmering dream. . . .

(0451-130480—$2.95 U.S., $3.50 Canada)

Buy them at your local bookstore or use this convenient coupon for ordering.
NEW AMERICAN LIBRARY
P.O. Box 999, Bergenfield, New Jersey 07621

Please send me the books I have checked above. I am enclosing $_____
(please add $1.00 to this order to cover postage and handling). Send check or money order—no cash or C.O.D.'s. Prices and numbers are subject to change without notice.

Name_____

Address_____

City _____ State _____ Zip Code _____
Allow 4-6 weeks for delivery.
This offer is subject to withdrawal without notice.